The Good Wolf

Derek Smith has lived most of his life in the East End of London. He has for many years been involved in community projects in the area as Writer-in-Residence for *Soapbox Theatre* in Newham, as one of the founders of *Page One* bookshop in Stratford and as a co-op development worker in Tower Hamlets. He has had plays performed on radio, television and the stage and had two novels published for children by Faber & Faber, *Hard Cash*, which was adapted for radio, and *Frances Fairweather Demon Striker!* which was short-listed for the Children's Book Award. A book for younger children, *The Magical World of Lucy-Anne*, was published by Walker Books.

Abi Bown comes from Liverpool where she studied Theatre and Art Design. She has worked as a designer in Young People's Theatre for ten years. Her illustrations have graced many theatre programmes and posters for Children's Theatre. *The Good Wolf* is her first book. Abi lives in the East End of London with her family.

D1380224

'I lay back and the three of them pushed me up the hill'

THE GOOD WOLF

Written by
Derek Smith

Illustrated by
Abi Bown

Earlham Books

Published in Great Britain
by Earlham Books
82 Earlham Grove
London E7 9AR

Made and printed by Redwood Books Ltd
Trowbridge, Wiltshire

Typesetting & design by Dan Leach

ISBN 0-9536283-0-2

Chapter 1

Da said she'd be coming this way – but where was she? Only one person had come along the path since I'd been here. And that was a woodcutter with an axe over his shoulder. I kept well out of his way.

I tried running on the spot to pass the time. That's difficult if you've got four legs, but not half so difficult as shadow-boxing. To do that you need to stand on two legs. Mind you I have been practising because it means you can reach things. Like wild cherries, or over a hedge into an orchard. Being on four legs is fine for running and chasing, but if you watch human beings you'll see they have their front paws free – and it occurred to me that maybe if mine were free I could do some of the things that they could do.

Well, it was worth a try. And if you are waiting in the woods – you've got to do something or you'll die of boredom.

So I practised getting up on two legs. For quite a while I kept stumbling and felt stupid. I was glad there was no one about to see. Imagine what Big Brother Ben would say! Or what my Da did in fact say when he saw me having a go a few days before:

'A wolf on two legs is less than half a wolf!'

And mentioning my Da – well there's no point hiding it. I had problems at home. Maybe it was boring in the woods, but at least no one was having a go at me. At home

I had Ma and Da, Big Brother Ben – and all the rest of my brothers and sisters. And that's not bringing in the rest of the pack. Joe Wolf is not the most popular of wolves.

Where was that girl?

I had been waiting so long I wondered whether Ma and Da had been messing me about. I wouldn't put it past my parents. Their idea of punishment. I had a good mind just to go back home – but then I'd only get a telling-off. What would be worse – being laughed at or a telling-off? So long as I don't get another lecture.

Wolves don't do this, don't do that. I've heard it all. I tried to tell Aunty next door that there had to be a first for anything – and you should have seen her jaw drop. 'Where would we be,' she said, 'if all wolves thought that?' Then she told me, because she wasn't really asking a question. 'No one would know what a wolf was, no one would know what a wolf should do. You can't keep changing things. Or there'll be trouble.'

I didn't look for trouble. I just got trouble. It just seemed to come. Like clouds in the sky.

Suddenly it clicked. I got the knack!

I was walking on my hind legs. I was wobbly but I could get about. I wanted to shout out – 'Look at me now! Look, look! I'm walking on my hind legs. I can manage it.' But there was no one to see. I had found the way to balance. If I didn't lean too far forward and not too far back, and pushed down with my back feet. I wished Ma and Da were here. Then I changed my mind. They wouldn't see the sense in it. Nor Big Brother Ben or Sister Sarah.

I found I could clap my paws. Well I could a bit if I didn't do it too hard. Then I had a rest against a tree. Two-leg walking really makes the calves hurt. I suppose that's natural, putting my full weight on just two legs – that's bound to be a strain. And how I wished I could show someone!

Don't you know that feeling? You've just learnt to do something new and you're dying to show someone, anyone… Well there was no one.

Till the girl came.

I first saw her coming down the path, some way off. She was dressed in red and had a little basket. I couldn't see her face because she had her hood up. She was walking steadily and hadn't seen me as I was watching from behind a tree.

I wondered how to get her into conversation. After all that was why I was here. It would never do to just frighten her off. I had to get some important information.

Suddenly I knew what to do. I stood up on my hind legs and walked out onto the path.

'Look at me! Look at me!' I shouted as I walked unsteadily towards her, my front paws held in front to balance me.

The girl stopped in the middle of the path, a hand to her mouth.

I wobbled on towards her. 'Bet you've never met a wolf who can do this!'

I could see she was undecided. Thinking about running but she probably realised I could catch her easily. I felt sorry for her in a way. She was so easy.

'Watch me clap my paws!'

I clapped them all right. Smacked them hard against each other; well that will teach me to show off as I lost my balance and fell forward. I was unable to get one of my legs out in time and banged my jaw on the ground. The thump went right through me. I am sure I heard my teeth rattle.

'You all right?' said the girl. She had come up to me and was looking down. I could see her face now. It was roundish with blue eyes, wisps of blonde hair stuck out from her hood.

'My jaw,' I moaned.

'You gave it quite a bang,' she said. 'But you were good. It was only when you tried to clap…'

I groaned and rubbed my jaw.

'Sit still awhile. It doesn't look broken.' She touched my jaw. 'I think it's all right. Open your mouth.' I did so and she looked inside. 'Your teeth look all right. No blood. Just sit still. Take a rest – you'll be all right in a minute.'

Well I certainly didn't feel like running about – so I lay out flat and rested my jaw in the dust.

'You know what you reminded me of when you were walking like that?' she said. 'Don't answer, rest your jaw. Well my dad's a woodcutter,' she said. 'He made me a pair of stilts. You looked a bit like me on stilts. When I first tried them I used to fall down a lot. Not much fun at all. Now I'm good – and I've got a big pair. Last Halloween I dressed up as a ghost – oh I did scare people looking in at them through their upstairs windows!'

She had a good laugh at this. And maybe I would have thought it funny if my jaw ached less.

'Oh poor you,' she said. 'Sorry. But I'm not making fun of you, just trying to cheer you up.'

I nodded. The ache was getting less although my lower teeth were throbbing. I lifted my head a little and shook it. Then opened my jaw and closed it. I did that several times.

'My mummy told me when I came out,' said the girl, 'she said I mustn't speak to anyone. She said there's some unpleasant characters about. She said I was to go as quickly as possible to Grandma's house.' Her hands went to her face. 'Oh I told you!'

'It's all right,' I said rubbing my jaw. 'Your secret is safe with me.'

'Are you sure?' she said.

'Well to tell you the truth,' I said, 'I was sent to meet you.'

She took a step backwards and looked at me warily. 'Sent to meet me? What for? By who?'

'My Da saw you leave your house. He said there was an opportunity…'

'For what?'

'What do wolves need opportunities for?' I said. 'One guess.

She thought for a second then blurted out, 'You mean you're going to eat me and Grandma?'

'It wasn't my idea,' I said.

'Oh please don't, Mr Wolf.'

'Joe,' I said.

'Please, Joe – I'm just taking some food to Grandma. She hasn't been very well you see. Mummy made her some scones, and I've got a few vegetables, and a pie… She's just an old lady.' Her voice faded, and she said very quietly, 'And I'm just a very young one.'

I didn't say anything. Wolves don't care how old anyone is. They don't ask for birth certificates.

'It's nothing personal,' I said. 'I'm a wolf. You must have read about wolves.'

She nodded.

'Da said I had to help out now. I couldn't just hang about the cave especially as he was slowed up because of being bitten by a bear. He said it was time I was more wolflike.'

She screwed up her eyes. 'You look enough like a wolf to me.'

Was it her eyes? Or the look on her face? But I just knew she wouldn't laugh. So I told her.

'Not enough like one,' I said. 'You see – I don't eat meat.'

'You mean you're a vegetarian.'

'No! No!' I declared. 'Please don't use that expression.'

'But if you don't eat meat then you're a...'

'Please don't say the V-word!'

'Sorry. It's just my aunty is a... you know. And no one minds. But then I can see for a wolf it's probably not the thing to be. I suppose your whole family eats meat?'

'And how!' I grimaced at the thought of it. 'But I can't stand it. Ma and Da are trying to cure me. They're trying to toughen me up. So I have to find out where you were going.'

'I told you.'

'Well you did make it rather easy. Then I have to get there before you...'

'And eat us.'

'Not all of you. I have to take as much as I can back.'

She was silent a little while then said, 'And are you going to?'

I took a deep breath, my jaw still ached a little. I got up and strode around, walking round and round the little girl. 'I tried to tell them it wouldn't work. They said force yourself. But to tell you the truth – I don't want to. Not now that I've met you.'

'I appreciate your difficulties, Joe.'

'I should though, you know. I really should force myself.'

'If you don't really want to, Joe – then don't.'

I looked at her. Killing her wouldn't be difficult. She was pretty little, and an old lady would be a piece of cake. But all that blood... Ooer! All that bone and gristle. Yuk!

I said, 'Go quick. Do what your mum says, go straight to Grandma's and don't talk to anyone. Go, hurry up – before I er... force myself.'

She came in close and gave me a kiss on the cheek. I don't know whether I liked it or not. I've never been kissed before. Wolves don't kiss.

'I'm off, Joe. Thank you. You don't look like you're going to force yourself.' she said. 'By-ee!' And with a wave she set off down the path.

And I went back to see Ma and Da.

Chapter 2

When I got back to the cave Ma and Da were quite grumpy as all they had had to eat was a couple of squirrels. And they got grumpier still when they saw I had nothing with me.

'I went to the woods,' I said. 'Where you said I should go. And she never came.' When neither of them said anything I added, 'A little girl in red you said. Well no one came at all. Not all the time I was there.'

'You sure?' said Da. 'I saw her take the path into the woods.'

'She must have strayed off it,' I said.

'You sure you went to the right place?' said Ma.

'Absolutely. 100 per cent.'

'I wish I was,' said Da.

'You're two years old now,' said Ma. 'Not a cub anymore. We expect you to be one of the breadwinners. Especially with your father injured and me in my condition...'

Ma was expecting a new litter. Da reckoned six or seven. She certainly was big and that made me feel extra guilty.

'I could get some blackberries,' I said and immediately wished I hadn't. For Da just exploded. He rose up with a savage growl and cuffed me repeatedly round the ears. I felt like a drum as he beat out his message.

'Blackberries! Did I hear you say *blackberries*!' Cuff,

cuff. 'I am a wolf!' Cuff. 'The son of a wolf.' Cuff. 'I don't eat blackberries!'

I sank into the ground. My ears were singing. This just wasn't going to be my day.

'Whoever heard such a thing!' joined in Ma and gave me a couple of cuffs.

The two of them were now up and about, going round and round my prone body.

'My family are grey wolves,' she went on as she circled. 'We have roamed from Siberia to Canada. Crossing the seas on ice floes. We have killed caribou, deer, bears, moose. And *he* has the cheek to offer *me* blackberries!'

'You're a joke,' said Da.

'It's not my fault,' I said miserably. 'You can't help what you are.'

'You can and you will,' said Da.

It was then big brother Ben came in the cave. When he saw me getting it – he stood back to enjoy it the more. Wishing only to join in.

'Why can't you be more like Ben?' said Ma, seeing him.

Big Brother Ben smirked.

'Other sons,' said Da, 'come back with meat. They don't offer to pick blackberries.'

'He's a veggie,' taunted Ben.

Ma turned on him. 'How many times have I told you about the V-word?'

'Sorry, Ma. But I didn't say all of it.' He lowered his head.

'I won't have bad language.'

'It's bad enough *him* being one,' said Da, 'without you saying it.'

'And to top it,' said Ma, 'he couldn't find the little girl in red.'

'Yes he could,' said Ben.

They both turned to big brother. And so did I. What did he know?

'I followed him,' said Ben. 'I saw him standing on his hind legs in the wood. He looked so silly. You should've seen him. Tottering about like a human baby. Then she came.'

Ma turned to me, 'I thought you said she didn't.'

'Ooh is that what he said?' said Ben. 'What a fibber! She came all right. And they had a chat. She told him she was going to Grandma's house…'

Dad's hair bristled on his neck. He snarled, 'This is beyond belief. My son! He speaks to her, he gets the information, and then he comes back – and lies!'

'What can you expect of a… of a thingummy-bob?' said Ben.

I cringed. I knew I was going to get it now.

'I had hopes,' said Da, 'that this time you might, for once, be a wolf!'

He was shaking his head. He was angry all right but I could also see he was sad. I might have disappointed him but I was still his son.

'*I* could go to Grandma's,' said Ben.

'Oh would you,' said Ma. 'That would be so nice of you. Isn't he a good boy?'

Ben smirked.

'I'd be so grateful,' said Ma. 'All we've had is squirrel today. And you know your Da is still recovering from that bear nip.'

'Grandma's here I come!' exclaimed Ben. And he was off out.

'Such a helpful boy,' sighed Ma.

'Unlike this one,' said Da.

'I don't know why he's turned out this way,' said Ma. 'There's no one in my family.'

'Nor mine,' said Da.

'It's so demeaning. I can't hold my head up in the pack anymore. I think we should kick him out. Let him fend for himself in the real world.'

'Is that what you want, lad?' growled Da, pushing his head up close to mine. I could see myself in the black of his eyes. I looked enough like a wolf. Why couldn't I be one?

'Gimme a chance,' I said. 'One chance. I'll show you what I am.'

'One chance,' said Da. 'Your last.'

Chapter 3

Ma and Da said I had to go off and visit a pig – and then come back with the bacon. Or else. At the same time Ma gave me an earful of how wonderful Ben was. *He* never had to be asked twice, *he* could always be relied on, that's why *he* was on his way to Grandma's to finish the job that I didn't have the stomach for.

All too true. My problem was I seemed to get involved with my victims, well what should be my victims, and then I didn't want to eat them. Whereas Ben would eat the little girl and her grandmother without a second thought. In some ways I felt envious of Big Brother Ben, the way he just didn't care, whereas I care too much about what I eat. I always have done, and I suppose that's why I've become a 'you know what'.

I know what you are going to ask. Well I would ask anyway. Why if I was a 'you know what' – was I going to kill a pig?

You can't get away from it; family is family. I wanted Ma and Da to think well of me. I didn't want them to curse me or feel disgraced by me. I wanted them to be able to hold up their heads in the pack. It was simple enough. Wolves eat meat, everyone knows that. And me being a wolf, if I wanted to keep my family – then I had to, too.

And this was my last chance. This time I would. I really would.

But before I dealt with the pig, I had somewhere else to go. Making sure I wasn't being watched – I set off for the woods. Once in them I began to sprint. This wasn't the time for messing around on two legs. Speed I wanted. I went flat out along the path, stretching my legs wide and long. I felt a hundred per cent wolf. What a runner! What speed!

I imagined it was a race, and in a way it was. I was leading the pack. I thought of myself with some of Ma's family in Canada full pelt across the ice and snow. I suppose they would be chasing deer or caribou but I didn't think about that side of it. Just the thrill of running with the wolves.

I was soon hot, my breathing laboured, but I pressed on without losing speed. I cut on to a smaller path where the woods were thick and the sun hardly shone through at all. I was making a frightful noise, brushing against bushes, pounding the ground, and my breath had become fierce and harsh. Suppose I met a bear? Too bad, I'd have to risk it. It was now a matter of life or death.

Finally I came out into the clearing and there in the sunshine was the little cottage. It had flowers round the front door and vegetables growing in the front patch. I got to the door and fell against it, utterly exhausted. With a weary paw I rapped.

In a few seconds the door opened.

Standing there was a young tall man with fair hair, wearing green and brown working-clothes. He looked very like the little girl in red I had met earlier. The instant he saw me he reached for the axe that was leaning against the wall. And suddenly I realised I hadn't thought this out. I could barely speak after my run. The man raised the axe. I was too tired to move, too tired to protest. I just closed my eyes and waited for the chopper to come down.

And waited.

It seemed a long time coming. When I opened my eyes the man was leaning on his axe, grinning. He had seen I couldn't do a thing and wondered what I was up to.

'Grandma's house,' I managed to say.

The man was suddenly alert. 'What?'

The words came out in a rush of breath. 'You must go to Grandma's. A wolf is on his way there.' I didn't say my brother. Such details only confuse things. 'Grandma…the little girl… Go. At once!'

I had barely finished when the man, axe in hand, was tearing down the path and across the clearing. Just before he entered the woods he turned and called to me:

'I'll remember you for this, good wolf!'

And then with long lanky strides he was off into the wood.

I stayed a little while outside the woodcutter's cottage, getting my breath back. I found some water in a bucket and round the back a pile of vegetables. I helped myself to some carrots and celery. And felt better for that. I just hoped the woodcutter would be in time. Although Big Brother Ben had a good start – the woodcutter knew the woods well. He might just make it.

I could imagine what Ben might be up to in that cottage. Oh that poor old lady! And then the little girl's turn. And I am sure he'd think of some wicked way to tease them. Before eating them up.

But there was nothing further I could do. I had a pig to meet.

Chapter 4

It was so laughable when I came to the pig's house. There it was in the middle of a field and made of straw. I mean really, there you are, a fat pig, every wolf in the district dying to get at you – so what do you do? Well you build a house. OK – that's sensible, but what do you build it of? Straw!

Let's get real.

He might as well as made it out of paper bags. He might as well have sat in a lion's cage with a tea towel over his head. He might as well have put his head in Da's mouth and given him the salt and pepper.

I went to the door of the house of straw and knocked on the door.

'Let me in, little pig,' I called.

'Go away!' came a voice from inside. 'I know what you are. And I know what you want. And I won't let you in.'

'This house couldn't stop me,' I said.

'Oh yes it can! I won't let you in.'

'Little pig,' I said, 'a house of straw is just stupid. It couldn't keep anyone out. Let alone a wolf.'

'Don't try to fool me. I am perfectly safe in here. Safe as houses.'

At that point I looked in through the window, and saw the little pig in a corner, his bum in the air and his head under a cushion.

I said, 'Look, little pig, I could blow this house down, you know.'

'You're just saying that,' said the pig, its tail wiggling as it spoke. 'I am safe as safe can be. This house could stand up to a hurricane.'

That was too much. How silly can you get!

I took a deep breath. Then I huffed and I puffed. And I blew the house down.

After the straw had cleared, and I had recovered from my blowing session, I saw the little pig in the corner – well where the corner had been, bum in the air, with the cushion still over his head. At least he'd been able to hold on to that. But his house was now scattered all over the field. It was sad really.

I went up to the little pig and took off his cushion.

'See?' I said.

'I see,' said the little pig, trembling like a fresh cooled jelly.

'Straw is useless.'

'Please don't eat me.'

'Straw is a waste of time.'

'I'm only a *little* pig.'

'Straw has no strength.'

'I'd hardly make a mouthful.'

'Why did you choose straw?' I asked.

The little pig was sitting on his bottom looking up at me, thinking I would spring any minute. And I was thinking that perhaps I should. After all that was why I had come. That was what Ma and Da wanted me to do.

'I didn't have any money,' said the pig, 'so I couldn't make a house of bricks. And my knife wasn't sharp enough to cut sticks. So all that left was straw.'

'But it's useless,' I said.

'I see it is now,' said the pig. 'I suppose I just hoped it wouldn't be.'

'Hope by itself isn't much good,' I said looking over the straw. I like problems, and this was an interesting one. Suppose all you had was straw. How could you keep a wolf out?

'Let's have a go,' I said, 'and see if we can make it stronger this time.'

The pig looked at me in disbelief. 'You mean you're not going to eat me?'

'I mean I am not going to eat you yet. And I'm not going to do all the work.'

The pig got up and the two of us gathered all the straw together in one place. Then I walked round and round that pile of straw, scratching my head for a good five or ten minutes. And the longer I walked round and round the more obvious it became that whatever you did with the straw you couldn't keep a wolf out.

'It's not going to work, is it?' said the pig miserably.

Then I had my idea.

'Let's build the house,' I said.

So we built it. The house when finished didn't look much different from one before. It certainly wasn't any stronger. But what it did have was a back door.

'You see,' I said to the little pig, 'any wolf who comes along can blow your house down. No matter what you do to it. So your only chance is to get out quick. As soon as the wolf starts huffing and puffing you have to be out the back door and running. Have you got somewhere to go?'

'Well my brother has a house of sticks.'

'Then get sprinting there as soon as the wolf takes his first big breath.'

I looked over the house, had a walk around inside and made sure the back door opened properly. I had enjoyed building it. I even felt a bit jealous; it was cosier than the cave we lived in. That was bare, apart from the bones lying about, while the little pig had furniture.

'Well I'd best be off,' I said.

'Aren't you going to eat me then?' said the pig.

'I want to know whether the back-door plan will work.'

And so I left him, feeling quite happy with my afternoon's work. It was only as a started to get near home that I began to think what I had done. Or rather what I had not done.

There was going to be another row.

Chapter 5

When I got back to the cave Ma and Da were laid out in the dust. I had been trying to think up a story; how the pig had escaped somehow. I was sure it would be the first thing they would asked me. But they didn't. In fact they hardly noticed me. I sat down and wondered what was going on.

In a little while Da shook his head and sighed. I looked to Ma. She sniffed, and I could see then that she had been crying. They've had an argument I thought. Best for me to keep out of it.

'He just volunteered,' said Ma almost to herself. 'He wanted to help us out.'

'He was a good lad,' said Da. 'Quite like me in some ways.'

'He had your eyes,' she sighed. 'Who'd have thought when he went out this morning that it would have come to this?'

By this time I was bursting with curiosity but I didn't want to say anything, or they would start asking me questions.

'He's a hero,' said Da. 'We'll always remember him that way. Brave, fearless…'

'He was my pride and joy,' sniffed Ma.

I couldn't keep out it. I had half an idea what it was about, and knew I had a fair bit to do with it.

'Has Ben had an accident?' I asked.

'At Grandma's house,' said Da with a sigh.

'Your Sister Sarah heard some shepherds talking about it,' joined in Ma.

'He had grandma locked in the cupboard,' said Da, 'And was about to pounce on the girl – when the woodcutter turned up.'

'What a bit of bad luck!' exclaimed Ma.

'Ben would've got away,' said Da. 'But you know how he is, likes a joke.'

'Lik*ed* a joke,' sighed Ma.

'Well he was wearing a long nightdress, pretending to be Grandma,' said Da, 'and the silly lad tripped up on it.'

'And the woodcutter chopped his head off.' Ma began to cry.

Da went to comfort her. And I was left with a lot to think about. Hadn't I sent the woodcutter to Grandma's in the first place? And what did I think he'd do? Well to tell you the truth I thought he would have just run Ben off. Well maybe a bit more, but I never expected him to chop Ben's head off. That was drastic.

'A hero he was,' said Ma.

'A hero he died,' said Da.

Ma turned to me, '*You* should have gone to Grandma's.'

'Yes, I should,' I said trying to sound as convincing as possible. 'I wish it had been me.'

'So do I,' said Ma.

'Now, now,' said Da.

'Well,' said Ma, 'if it wasn't for this…' she hesitated then said the word she had always forbidden us to use, 'this *vegetarian* – then Ben would be alive.'

I could see Da was shocked.

'Let's not say things we might regret.'

'I have lost my first born son. While this…' She was unable to repeat the word, 'This… one lives.' Seething, she held me in her dark eyes. 'If you want to defend him – ask him where the pig is.'

Da looked at me. I looked away.

'Da…' I said.

'Don't say a thing,' he said.

'I can't help what I am.'

'You can,' said Ma. 'But you won't.'

'Why won't you accept me for what I am?' I looked from one to the other. 'Ma? Da? Please!'

There was a long silence. I wanted Da to come to my aid, to speak up for me. I wanted him to tell me that I was all right. I wanted him to persuade Ma. I wanted to be told that I belonged. I wanted a soft word, a word of comfort.

'You'd better go,' said Da.

I looked at the coldness of his jaw and knew there was nothing I could say. I turned to Ma.

'What are you waiting for?' she said sharply.

I got up and left.

Chapter 6

I wandered off hardly knowing where I was going. I had been kicked out by my family and had nowhere to go. Wolves don't make friends easily. You've heard of lone wolves – well that was me now. I was on my own.

But even if you are lonely you have to eat. I followed the hedgerows eating blackberries, no matter what Da thought of them. Then I found an orchard. I managed to get through the hedge, and this is where my new-found skill of walking on my hind legs came in useful. By standing on two legs I could reach the apples, some with my jaw, and some I could knock off with my front paws.

I had a good feed and that made me feel less unhappy. There's nothing like a full stomach for that. At least, I thought, it was still summer, and if you are going to get thrown out – then that was the best time for it. Midwinter would be awful; just contemplating the cold and dark made me shudder.

I was almost ready to leave the orchard when I heard a shout.

'Oi – you!'

I turned and saw a portly, bald-headed farmer heading towards me. In the sunshine his head shone but that wasn't the only thing that shone, for in his hands he had a shotgun. He was now running in his clumpy boots. I dropped onto four legs and sprinted in panic.

I got to the hedge and looked frantically for the hole I had come in by. I ran up and down, trying to find it.

'Bang!'

At the same instant I had found the hole and was through. But I was not quite quick enough – for the sudden pain in my back foot told me I'd been hit. Once through the hedge I limped off for cover. I went through a gate into a field of cows; they all drew away from me. Not that I cared less about them, but they weren't to know that.

My injured leg was certainly slowing me down so I kept in close to the hedge. I went through into some more fields. Sheep ran off, bleating miserably. Then in another field, halfway across, I spotted a bull. He was a huge brown beast with sharp looking horns. He was watching my every movement. If I hadn't have been injured he wouldn't have been a problem. A bull could never catch a healthy wolf. I could tie him in knots. But I wasn't healthy. The best thing I could do was pretend I was, and move confidently, at the same time keeping an eye on him.

Carefully I crossed the field. Even from this distance I could hear him snorting and pawing the ground. I went steadily on, trying not to attract attention, my injured leg dragging – and hoping I would make it to the other side.

Then he charged. The ground shook as he came, thundering along on the short dry grass. I ran as best I could – but it wasn't much of a run. Too slow, too laboured – and the bull knew he had me.

I stopped and I faced the charging animal. Its head was down, its horns forward and it was almost on me. I waited until the last instant, and then I stepped aside. The bull missed me and ran past.

'Stay in one place!' he bellowed as he turned.

I backed off. The way out of the field was still some way off, but not so far was a haystack. If I could get to it...

I dodged the next charge, but the bull was closer.

'Stay where you are, coward!' roared the bull.

This time he hadn't gone so fast and was expecting a dodge. I backed away, getting closer to the stack. The tips on those horns were terrifying, like knives. The bull was turning quicker, he was getting my measure.

I faced him again for the next charge. I let him thunder as close as I dared, horns thrusting. Then when the bull was barely a metre away I kicked up dust and stepped aside. The bull ran past me by a hairsbreadth. He pulled up and shook his head, then again and again. I had done what I wanted to and got dust in its eyes.

'That's not fair! Cheat!' he yelled as he ran round and round, furiously twisting his head.

I had long enough to get to the haystack before he

came for me again. By then I was on top. The bull wandered about me. He didn't batter the stack but had no intention of letting me get off.

'I'm not going anywhere,' he said sourly.

And he wasn't. I stayed on the stack for the rest of that hot afternoon. I licked my injured back paw which had pellets of shot in it and watched the bull circle round.

At last, near sunset the farmer came. The same bald farmer who had shot me. I lay low on the haystack and made not a sound. The bull was lead away and out of the field. When all was quiet I came down. I could have slept there but I was worried the bull might come back in the morning and surprise me. Then I'd be trapped for another day.

I went into a field where a stream flowed through. I drank and bathed my injured limb. And then found a clump of bushes where I could spend the night.

Chapter 7

In the morning my leg was worse. So I rested up in the bushes. I couldn't sleep as my wound hurt, so I just lay, hoping the pain would go away. The day was hot and still, with only the flies to cause me a nuisance. I saw no one.

By late morning I began to get thirsty. I stayed for as long as I could without a drink but by mid afternoon I could go no longer. I had to have water.

I dragged myself down to the stream. It was a bumpy, painful journey – it was as if my injured leg was a cartload I had to pull. By the time I got there I was exhausted. I drank my fill and lay out in the shallow part of the stream. The cool water eased my leg.

There was a tree overhead which gave some shade. If I was in good health, it would have been perfect, but with my injury – I was too much in the open. If the farmer came – I wouldn't be able to escape this time. I needed to hide, but was so comfortable lying in the stream that I didn't want to move.

It was when I heard whistling that I knew I had stayed too long. I pricked up my ears. The sound was a little way off but coming my way. I heaved myself out of the stream. There was no point trying to get away; the country was too open. So I hid behind the tree and hoped whoever was whistling would simply wander by.

And then a pig came into sight, a pink pig carrying a bucket. As it came closer I realised it was the pig whose house was made of straw. I wondered what he was doing round here – as surely we weren't close to his house.

As the pig came by the tree, whistling and swinging the bucket, I came out.

'Hello, little pig.'

The pig jerked in surprise.

'It's me,' I said.

'Thank Heavens,' said the pig, patting its chest with relief. 'I thought you were a wolf. I mean… well you know, an ordinary wolf.'

'Yes, I know.'

The pig smiled at me smugly. 'The back-door thing worked.'

'Why what happened?'

'I got a visit from a wolf. Like you but it had a white patch on its head.'

My sister Sarah, I thought. Ma and Da must have sent her to finish off the job.

'While it was huffing and puffing, I was off out the back door and along to my brother's house. The one with the house of sticks.'

'Is that where you are now?'

'Oh no. His house got blown down too. But we used your idea again. The wolf didn't come for a few hours and we had time to make a back door. Then when the wolf came and did its huffing and puffing – we got out and went to my older brother who has a house of bricks.'

'That's more like it,' I said. 'Bricks.'

'It's just over there. Why don't you come over for some tea?'

'I'd love to.'

'Just got to get some water,' said the pig and went down to the stream to fill the bucket. When it was full he came back to me and we set off.

'Just over that hill,' the pig pointed out. 'Why you're hurt.'

'A farmer shot me.'

'Do you think you can make up the hill?'

'It's rather steep,' I said. The cooling effect of the water had worn off and I was hobbling again.

'Stay here then. I'll get my brothers.'

I attempted to carry on walking.

'Please stay,' said the pig. 'You helped me, now it's my turn to help you.'

I didn't need to be asked again, my leg was aching too much. I sank onto the ground.

'Back in a minute,' said the pig.

I watched him climb the hill, swinging the bucket. The sky was very blue and it looked like he was walking into the sun. He was a very nice fellow, but I thought him rather careless. But then would you expect anything else of a pig who built a house of straw?

He disappeared over the brow, and a few minutes later I saw three pigs appear. One of them was my friend, the pink pig, another was black and the third was pink and black. It occurred to me that their parents were probably a pink pig and a black pig. The black pig was pushing a wheelbarrow. It seemed almost to be running away from him down the hill.

When they got to me my pig introduced the others.

'I'm Pinky,' he said. 'This is Inky.' That was the black pig. 'And that's Ponky.' That was the pink and black pig.

'Pleased to meet you,' I said. 'I'm Joe.'

'We've heard all about you,' said Inky. 'And now we must get you to our house quickly.'

''To our house quickly,' said Ponky.

'We think the wolf is coming soon,' said Inky.

'Coming soon,' said Ponky.

They bundled me into the wheelbarrow. There was a cushion in it to make it softer, and I was pleased at the thoughtfulness. I lay back and the three of them pushed the barrow up the hill. It was hard work for them, they were only little pigs, and I could see the sweat breaking out on their foreheads. But there was nothing I could do to help, and was grateful when they reached the top. From there, down the other side, I could see the little house of bricks.

In the front was a small garden with a low wooden fence round it. That wouldn't keep anyone out I thought, but then I thought perhaps it's for decoration. Wolves are not used to that sort of thing. We lead very plain lives. As we drew closer I could see rows of vegetables, and to one side a row of bean poles with runner beans and scarlet flowers just beginning to twine round.

When they got me to the house they helped me in over the step, and I was put to bed and given vegetable soup. While I rested Inky had a look at my leg.

'It's got bits of lead shot in it,' he said.

'Lead shot in it,' said Ponky.

'We should try to get it out,' said Inky. 'It'll hurt.'

'Hurt,' said Ponky.

Inky had built the house and I realised almost at once that he was the cleverest of the three. He talked sense. Pinky was a good chap but anyone who built a house of straw had to have a strange view of life, while Ponky just seemed to repeat all that Inky said, which showed, if nothing else, a lack of originality.

'Do what you have to,' I said.

Inky got a knife and some needles which he first boiled in a saucepan. I was impressed by that, I certainly wouldn't have thought of boiling them.

'To sterilise them,' he said.

Then over about an hour he prised out from my leg about a dozen tiny balls of lead shot. And he was right. It did hurt. I had to hold onto the bed to stop from crying out. Imagine that! A wolf squealing in the company of three little pigs. Well I have some pride but I must say I was awfully glad when the last bit of lead shot was out. My leg was raw with pain when he washed it. Just touching it made me squirm. At last he wrapped it in bandage – and I sighed with relief that it was all over.

I was then tucked in bed and given some herb tea. I don't know what was in that tea, but whatever it was soon put me to sleep.

Chapter 8

I was woken by a knock on the door followed by a gruff voice trying to speak kindly. 'Little pigs, little pigs, please let me in!'

Everything in that house stopped dead. Inky had been reading, Pinky peeling vegetables and Ponky doing the washing. The rapping at the door and the attempt at kindliness fooled no one. We all knew who it was. Even Pinky.

Inky whispered, 'Stay calm, it can't get in.'

'Can't get in,' nodded Ponky.

'I do hope so,' said Pinky, 'but it certainly made a mess of my house.'

The knocking on the door was repeated. This time a little more violently. 'Little pigs, little pigs, let me in.'

'No,' shouted Inky.

'No,' said Ponky.

'No' whispered Pinky.

A nose came through the letter box which I instantly recognised as my sister Sarah's nose. And she said in her sweetest voice: 'Please, little pigs, I've come a long way and I'm ever so hungry.'

The little pigs looked at each other, and felt even less comfortable now that my sister Sarah had informed them how hungry she was. Well who could blame them for that?

'Sarah!' I called from the bed, 'Would you please go away!'

'Who's that?' said the nose twitching and sniffing about.

'It's your brother Joe,' I said.

'Oh my dear brother Joe,' said Sarah. 'How I am longing to see you! Please let me in, little pigs. I do so want to see my little brother.'

'No!' called the three little pigs.

'Fancy denying a sister from seeing her favourite brother. How cruel you are!' She gave a mock weep followed by a few seconds silence. Then she said, 'Brother Joe – why not come out and see me?'

'I've hurt my leg,' I said, and immediately realised I shouldn't have told her, because she would now know I wouldn't be a lot of help to the pigs.

'Oh my poor little brother! Now little pigs, you must allow a family visit. I have some flowers and a box of chocolates.'

I shook my head and whispered, 'She's lying.'

'And a bunch of grapes, and a book.'

When she got no answer she said, 'I know you are a little bit suspicious of me, little pigs, so suppose I just leave them all on the step. Then I'll go away – and you can come out and get them.'

Her nose was retracted from the letter box.

After a few seconds Pinky said, 'She's gone. Goody – we can get the chocolates.'

'Of course she hasn't,' said Inky. 'She's just waiting for one of us to open the door. Then she'll push him aside and be in.'

'And be in,' said Ponky.

'Well shall I just go outside and have a look?' said Pinky.

'Most definitely not,' said Inky.

'Not,' said Ponky.

'Then how will we know whether she has gone or not?' said Pinky.

'She hasn't gone,' I said.

'I heard that,' said a voice from outside. 'Take no notice of my lying brother. I have gone!'

'See, she's gone,' said Pinky.

Inky sighed. I shrugged. I could understand now how Pinky had come to build a house of straw.

'Then who is speaking?' asked Pinky anxiously.

'Is speaking?' said Ponky.

Pinky scratched his head and walked around in a circle. Round and round he went, trying to finger out the conundrum. Then suddenly he said:

'She's speaking!' And then like a light going on it came to him. 'She hasn't gone at all!'

Inky laughed and said to me, 'He may be slow but Pink gets there in the end.'

Perhaps, I thought, but he wouldn't last long without his brother.

'Go away!' shouted Pinky through the letter box. 'You can't trick us. We're too clever for you!'

The reply was a shaking of the door. 'Let me in, little pigs. I must see my poor sick brother. Boo hoo hoo!'

'Well I don't want to see you,' I called, not fooled at all by the tears.

'I've got a message from mother,' she said.

'Post it to me.'

Then the door began to shake and tremble as Sarah threw her weight against it. 'Let me in, little pigs, or I'll huff and I'll puff and I'll blow your house down.'

'A waste of time,' called Inky. 'These are finest sandstone brick!'

'Sandstone brick!' said Ponky.

'And it'll take more than a bit of wolf's breath to blow them down!'

'Blow them down!' said Ponky.

The bashing against the door stopped. We listened and could hear nothing. I wished I was able to get up and help out but I felt rather useless, and I must say somewhat ashamed of the tactics used by wolves. Well it is different seeing them from the inside. Seeing just how sneaky we can be.

'Has she gone?' whispered Pinky.

'No,' I said. 'She's getting her breath together. Any second she'll…'

I didn't have time to finish for suddenly there was a fierce wind. Everything in the house shook. A plate came off the table and broke, some bits and pieces came flying off the mantelpiece and the curtains fluttered like sails. But when the wind stopped, apart from the broken china and the things off the mantelpiece the house was intact. We still had four good walls and a roof.

'Thank heavens for that!' said Inky.

'Heavens for that!' said Ponky.

'She'll try again,' I said.

And she did. Three times in fact. Each time the wind was a little stronger but the house was stronger still. It was plain that, blow as she might, my Sister Sarah could make no impression on this house of bricks.

The pigs were jubilant and did a little dance. They held hands and circled round singing:

'*Who's afraid of the big bad wolf, big bad wolf? Who's afraid of the big bad wolf, big bad wolf? Oh no not me!*'

I said, 'It's not over yet.'

They stopped dancing.

'What do you think she'll do?' said Inky.

'Think she'll do,' said Ponky.

I lay back and put myself in Sarah's position.

'Well,' I said, 'if I couldn't blow the house down – then I'd come down the chimney.'

'Good job we've got a wolf here,' said Inky.

'Wolf here,' said Ponky.

Inky quickly got the others organised. There was a little fire in the grate but not much to worry a wolf. Pinky piled wood on the fire to build it up while Inky and Ponky filled up a large cooking-pot with water. They put this on the fire.

I don't really want to tell you what happened next. After all the story is very well known. I dare say you have read about it in the paper or perhaps seen it on TV. It was all very sad. Maybe my sister and I didn't get along all that well but family is family. I nearly called out at the last minute, when I could hear her coming down the chimney. I could see her feet and wanted to shout, 'Sarah! Please go – before you get boiled alive!'

But as you know I didn't. When all is said and done I know how wolves think, and I knew that Sarah would not give in. If I warned her she would simply have another go. That's the way wolves are. It was her or the three little pigs.

The story in the paper of course says nothing about me being in the house. Well I asked the pigs to keep me out of it. I said my family thought badly enough of me already without Ma and Da knowing I had a part in Sister Sarah's end. So officially it was just the three little pigs, but now you know I had a part in it.

I would rather you kept it to yourself if you don't mind. You might think that Sarah had it coming to her but most wolves won't agree. They'll side with her, and I don't want to wake up one night and have to face a wolf pack.

I can tell you this – it most certainly wouldn't be a fair trial.

Chapter 9

The three little pigs decided to have a party to celebrate their victory over the wolf. And so they sent out lots of invitations to their friends and relations.

In the meantime the pigs were sharing one bed and I was in two of them put together. I wasn't happy about this and suggested I sleep on the floor, but they wouldn't have that.

'Not while you are recovering from injury,' said Inky.

'Recovering from injury,' added Ponky.

I was taking up a lot of space in their small house but there was little I could do about it. I couldn't make myself any smaller and my leg would recover in its own good time. So I lay in bed and made the most of it.

I also noted they were spending a lot of time feeding me. They were three *little* pigs and I was a big wolf – and I do have a healthy appetite. Their bowls were too small for me for a start; I could eat three or four of them and still feel hungry. In the end they gave me a washing up bowl to eat out of, and I know they had to go quite a way to gather the fruit and vegetables that I ate.

I knew this was only temporary. As soon as I was better I would be able to gather my own food.

But it was so good to be amongst friends. To not be teased by brothers and sisters, to not be told off by Ma and Da. It was so good to be somewhere where I was trusted and where for the first time in my life I could be myself without lying or pretending.

If I hadn't injured my leg I could have skipped for joy.

Over the next week I began to get better. I could hobble out to the front and sit there on fine days and watch the pigs working in their vegetable garden. They worked very hard, hoeing and planting. And perhaps they had to, with such a big guest.

Well that would change as soon as I was well and could get my own food. And why not get some for my three little friends too? Then I'd be repaying them for all their help.

Lying out in the sunshine I could imagine staying in that little brick house for the rest of my days. In a year or two one of them might get married, then they'd have piglets – and I could see myself as a sort of favourite uncle. Bouncing the little ones upon my knee, playing football with the bigger ones, and generally protecting them all.

At last I had found the right place to live.

The replies to the invitations started coming back, and it was only when I saw some lying about that I saw they were all refusals. Every one of their friends and relatives had some important reason why they couldn't come to the three little pigs' party.

'They do live some way off,' said Inky.

'Some way off,' said Ponky.

But I caught a shiftiness in their eyes which made me wonder. And this was confirmed one day when I was in the house on my own. The three little pigs had gone out to gather food from the hedgerows and I was reading in bed.

There was a knock on the door.

'Who is it?' I called.

'Cousin Alfred,' came a pig's voice.

I didn't know who Cousin Alfred was but I assumed he was a cousin of the pigs. And at last here was a pig who was taking up the invitation.

'Come in,' I called. 'The door isn't locked.'

The door swung open and there at the door was a pig in sailor's uniform carrying a kit bag over his shoulder.

'How do you,' I said and extended a paw.

But my friendly welcome was to no avail. Cousin Alfred took one look at me and let out a yell. Then he turned and ran as fast his little legs would carry him, all the time crying, 'Wolf! Wolf! There's a wolf!'

Through the open doorway I watched him. He must have broken every pig world record. Not once did he look back but just ran on as if he feared being torn limb from limb and eaten for breakfast. I sighed. If only he had given me time to explain what I was doing there and how I wasn't the usual sort of wolf.

Pinky was the first to come back, he was carrying a large bowl of blackberries. When I told him about Cousin Alfred he didn't seem at all surprised.

'It's what any pig would do,' he said.

Just then Inky and Ponky arrived, and suddenly I knew why no one was coming to their party.

'It's me,' I said. 'Isn't it? They won't come to a house with a wolf in it.'

The three little pigs didn't answer, and so I knew it was true.

'Don't they understand I am not that sort of wolf?' I looked to them all but the three of them were trying to avoid my eyes.

At last Inky said, 'They have all lost relatives to wolves.'

'Lost relatives to wolves,' said Ponky.

'But I'm different.'

'They say you're bound to say that,' said Pinky and held up a letter which did say that.

'But I have never killed a pig!'

'Not yet,' said Inky holding up another letter.

'Not yet,' said Ponky.

'But you know,' I said. 'You know I wouldn't do anything. You know I don't eat meat.'

Inky was gazing down at his paws looking most uncomfortable.

'We're very grateful,' he said, 'for all the help you have given us.'

'Have given us,' said Ponky.

'Very grateful,' mumbled Pinky.

'But suppose you turned on us?' said Inky.

'Turned on us?' said Ponky.

'But you know I wouldn't,' I declared.

But from the silence that followed I could see they didn't know that. It was then I began to see matters from their point of view. I was bigger than the three of them put together. And wasn't I living in their house? I could eat them all when they were asleep. Who was to say I wouldn't go berserk at their party, that was if they had one and that didn't look likely.

Looking at the three of them for the first time I understood clearly. The three little pigs didn't trust me.

'From the cradle,' said Inky, 'we have been told stories about wicked wolves.'

'Wicked wolves,' said Ponky.

'We have friends and relatives who have been eaten,' said Pinky.

'There's no end of tricks a wolf might try,' said Inky.

'A wolf might try,' said Ponky.

'But...' I began and stopped. Whatever I said could sound like a trick. Just a way of persuading them that I was the one good one.

'How do we really know about you?' said Inky.

'About you,' said Ponky.

I made one last try. 'But didn't I tell you what to do

when my Sister Sarah came? Didn't I help you with your house of straw?'

Pinky and Ponky looked a little shamefaced but Inky shook his head.

'It could be,' he said, 'that you are worse than all of them.'

'Worse than all of them,' said Ponky.

'It could be,' he said, 'that you are even prepared to sacrifice your own sister to get us.'

'To get us,' said Ponky.

I looked from one to the other. They were all so small. They had lived their lives in fear of wolves. How could I expect them to accept me? History was against me. Every wolf that had ever been was against me.

'I'll go,' I said.

'While you're injured you can stay,' said Inky.

'Can stay,' said Ponky.

'You can't do us much harm for the moment,' went on Inky. 'But soon as you are recovered…'

'Are recovered,' said Ponky.

'You've got to go.'

'Got to go,' said Ponky.

I stayed two more days with the three little pigs. They were no longer comfortable or happy days. I wasn't trusted. I wanted to be their friend but they were afraid to be mine.

The next night I saw they were keeping a watch on me through the night. They were staying awake in shifts. Not surprising, for as my leg got better then in their eyes I got more dangerous. Pinky took the first shift, then when he went to sleep, Ponky took over, and the last shift was taken by Inky. They sat in an armchair with a nightlight, just to watch me.

I decided I could stay no longer.

After breakfast the next day the three little pigs left the house to gather food. Now I decided was the time. I didn't want to stay for goodbyes. That would be embarrassing for them and me. I wasn't quite fully recovered – but I could certainly walk.

I left a note on the table:

> *Thank you for your help. I understand why*
> *this can't work. Best Wishes for a safe future.*
>
> *Joe Wolf*

Then I left the house of bricks.

Chapter 10

I walked most of that morning. I wanted to get out of the range of the three little pigs. They had asked me to go and for the time being I didn't want to see them. I didn't want to go into a field and find them there picking fruit or having a picnic. It would be awkward for them and for me.

I just wanted to get away from everyone I knew. Then I wouldn't have to keep explaining about myself. Apologising or telling lies. It was a lot easier to be just a wolf on my own.

I was feeling sorry for myself. No one wanted me. My own company was the best company. Or at least the only company I could rely on.

I found walking no problem. When I tried to run my back leg began to ache and in a short while I just had to stop. It was getting better but I wasn't up to full strength yet. I just hoped I wouldn't meet anyone that would make me run.

Well that wasn't to be.

About midday I stopped to eat. I found a field of carrots next to a field of turnips. I pulled out a couple of each and looked for somewhere safe to eat them. Certainly not in the middle of a field. Not far away I saw a cliff and I headed for it. The day had become quite hot with the sun overhead in a cloudless sky. I could do with some shade and some water.

I had hoped there was a cave in the cliff but I was disappointed. I grew up in caves and maybe it was just as well I didn't find one. Being there on my own would only remind me of my family who had thrown me out. Apart from that, it can be dangerous being in a cave on your own, especially if there is only one way out.

But I did find a stream, that seemed somehow to come out of the cliff. It was shallow and slow moving, and only about as wide as an easy leap. I sat in it and drank. It was good to cool my body, to have the water flowing over me in the warmth of the sun. I munched my carrots, took a drink, munched a bit of turnip, and thought that perhaps life wasn't so bad.

It was when I went to take another drink that I saw a shadow. It blocked out my reflection in the water. I froze and the hairs stiffened on the back of my neck. I watched the reflection, it was difficult to make out what it was, other than that it was big. The problem with water is that it confuses smells especially if there's a breeze.

I turned my head slowly. A little way off, coming in gently as if wearing carpet slippers, was a bear. It growled in annoyance when it saw me watching.

'Darn. I thought I could get you straight off.'

I began to back off down the stream, keeping the bear in sight. It was brown and shaggy, with a squat head and very powerful jaw. The bear entered the stream and came for me steadily, its great arms hanging slightly in front of its barrel of a body.

I didn't want to run, because that would simply show the bear that I couldn't run very far. I stopped, the bear stopped. It grinned at me.

'Nice day for a paddle,' he said.

'Lovely,' I said.

'You left your picnic behind.' The bear had stopped near the vegetables I had left. 'We could share it.'

'I've had enough, thank you very much. You have it.'

The bear picked up a carrot and threw it. 'Catch!'

I ducked out of the way and kicked some water at the bear. He kicked some back. We splashed each other lightly. It seemed very friendly, but I knew it wasn't. The bear just wasn't sure he could outrun me and so wanted to trick me instead. But I knew he could catch me, my leg wasn't up to a chase.

And I had to make sure that brown bruiser didn't find out.

'Hey wolf!' he called, beckoning with his arm. 'Why don't you come here? We could play... er water polo.'

'My mother told me *never* to play with bears.'

'But surely you don't always do what your mother says?' He had a teasing grin which showed an awful lot of strong teeth.

'Water polo isn't my game,' I said, knowing how such a game would end up. 'What about a game of football?'

The bear scratched its head. 'Football? With just two of us?'

'Well,' I said matter of factly, 'you go and get your team and I'll go off and get mine.'

The bear thought for a second and then said, 'I don't know enough bears.'

'Five aside then.'

Suddenly a large grin came over the bear's face. 'I think you'll just run away.'

'Why should I run from a nice friendly fellow like you?'

'Football is for sissies anyway,' he said.

I thought for a second. 'OK. Hide and Seek?'

'Yeh! You close your eyes and count fifty…'

I knew if I closed my eyes I was a goner. 'I can't count fifty.'

'Thirty then.'

'I can't count at all.' I looked very shamefaced.

'Not count at all? You've been badly brought up, wolf.'

'Show me how to count.'

'It's easy. It goes like this… One, two, three, four, five…'

I let him go on a bit then said, 'Brilliant! You certainly know how to count. But I am sure it is quite another thing doing it with your eyes shut.'

'Easy!'

'Don't believe it.'

'I've been doing it since I was a cub. Watch.' The bear closed his eyes and began to count. 'One, two, three…'

'Close 'em properly!'

And that was the last thing I said to the bear.

You can get quite a way in fifty seconds.

Chapter 11

Some way ahead I could see a church steeple and around it a cluster of houses. There was obviously a town ahead. But behind me I had a bear and I decided that I would go as close as possible to the town. That would frighten off the bear, and then hopefully I could skirt around the town.

I was making my way along a path that crossed a field. Coming over a stile I saw an old man. He was bent over his walking stick and wore a battered old hat. I decided not to hide. An old man couldn't do me much harm and I could smell bear. He wasn't too far behind.

The old man made his tottery way up to me whistling something only he knew the tune of. When he came close he called out:

'Good dog.' He stopped. 'I can see you are well trained. Let's see what I've got for you.'

He put his hand in his crumpled trousers and pulled out a dog biscuit, then held it out for me. I sniffed it. It was plainly made of crushed bones. I certainly wasn't going to touch that.

'Fussy dog eh? I wonder what you eat.'

Then something made him peer closely at me. He put a hand in his inside pocket and got out his glasses. He put them on and instantly threw up his hands.

'A wolf! You ain't a dog at all! A wolf!'

Then he dropped his stick, turned and ran, yelling, 'Wolf! Wolf!'

To see him go, back across that stile you would wonder he needed the stick at all. I could hear him through the hedgerow where all I could see were his hands waving, and making very good speed.

'A wolf! A wolf!' he continued crying to anyone who would hear.

I changed direction realising that the old man would certainly have warned anyone the way he was going. I thought of turning about but I caught a glimpse of brown behind a tree, and thought that I could probably deal with human beings better than I could deal with a bear.

I went over a stile and there just before me was a milk maid. She had a white pinafore dress and a soft white hat. Over her shoulders she carried a yoke, at either end of which were two buckets full of milk. She too took me for a dog, for a second that is, and gave me a smile, but she wasn't as short-sighted as the old man.

'A wolf! A wolf!' she cried.

She instantly dropped her yoke and turned about, running for all she was worth and yelling for all the world to hear.

'A wolf! A wolf!'

This place certainly didn't make me feel welcome.

I watched the milkmaid fleeing. Well she could certainly run, and she could shout too. She seemed a nice girl with her red cheeks, and I'd hoped in that instant of the first smile that we might have had a chat. Instead she was already in the next field where I could no longer see her but I could hear her words of warning.

I inspected her buckets. One had tipped over but the

other was upright, so I had a quick drink. It was beautiful creamy milk, no doubt fresh from the cow. Pity to leave it to waste. I drank some more. There was so much luscious cream at the top… A wolf doesn't get that very often.

I would have loved to stay and drink it all. But with milkmaids and old men crying wolf and a bear behind me I had to reluctantly leave it. Few things have left me sadder than that pail of milk I had to leave behind.

I looked over the stile in the direction I had come. There was the bear trying to hide in the hedgerow. He'd finish off the milk. That made me angry and I was about to tip it over, when I realised it was far better he have the milk for his dinner than have me. It would give me time to get away, and might even mean he'd forget about me completely.

So I continued on my way, taking a different direction across the field to the one the milkmaid had taken. I kept quite low down, being unsure what was in front and knowing full well what was behind.

Presently the bear climbed the stile and spotted the pail of milk. I sighed as I watched him drink. All that lovely cream wasted on that brute. His muzzle had gone white and I could hear him greedily slurping even at the distance I was.

A gate opened just in front of me, and there coming through was a farmer pushing a wheelbarrow full of beetroot. He wore wellington boots over his trousers, and a waistcoat with a pocket watch. His check hat was on the heap of beetroot in the barrow.

He came too fast for me to hide, and so for a few seconds we just looked at each other. And I knew what he would do after that. It seems the thing that all human beings do when they see my kind.

'A wolf! A wolf!' he cried and threw up his hands.

He then turned, left the wheelbarrow, leaped over the gate with amazing energy for someone his age, and was back off down the path he had come, yelling those unoriginal words.

At this point I wasn't too sure what to do. I had a bear behind me still busily drinking milk, three people had run off yelling 'wolf'. It was unlikely that no one would take any notice. I decided to wait where I was a while. I had my eye on the bear, he was busy but I knew things must be happening up ahead.

And they were.

It wasn't very many minutes later that I saw a crowd of people coming along the path where the milkmaid had fled. She was in front pointing. I could see men and women with brooms and hoes. I could see angry shotguns shaken in the air. The whole crowd of them were yelling and striding forward with the milkmaid at their head.

I kept absolutely still. They weren't coming in my direction, but I could plainly see whose direction they were going in. And if that creature hadn't had its head in a bucket and wasn't taken over by the delicious taste of that fresh creamy milk – it wouldn't have been waiting for them.

I think they saw him first.

'That's not a wolf, that's a bear.'

'She can't tell the difference!'

'Fancy calling a bear a wolf!'

Not that that stopped them marching on. The bear suddenly became aware of the hullabaloo and stopped licking the inside of the bucket. He looked, he saw, he ran.

Shotguns blasted. Followed by a hundred trampling feet, and the screams and yells of the townsfolk. Off they all ran across the field in the wake of the bear who I could no longer see because of the wall of people in front.

In a little while the field was empty. I could hear the yells and shots from the direction they had gone. I lay still and listened until I judged they were far enough off.

I allowed myself a smile of satisfaction. The bear was most definitely out of harm's way, and the town would be half empty too.

I would find somewhere I could lay up.

Chapter 12

I rested in a barn for a few hours. I meant to leave in the afternoon but when I went to go out I saw all the people coming back from the bear hunt. And I immediately ran back inside the barn. I scrambled up a ladder which took me to a hay loft where there was a small window above the barn door.

Keeping to one side in the shadows, I watched the people returning. They were in jubilant mood, singing and cheering. A little later there came, tied upon a pole, the body of the bear. It was carried by three men at either end while children ran alongside, daring each other to touch the bear, even though it was well and truly dead.

This was no time for a wolf to come out.

I would have to wait until nightfall. Until everyone was back in their houses eating and preparing for bed.

I wished then I had been more choosy about the barn I had picked. This one was near a farmhouse with a few other outbuildings. Not far away were some cottages. When I had come I had got the wrong impression. It had been so quiet because everyone had been out on the hunt. Now it was a hive of activity.

In the farmyard below me they were building a bonfire. A young boy was trying to help. He had red hair that looked like it had never seen a comb and a freckly face. He wore dark blue dungarees patched at the knees, with a fresh rip that left doubt whether it could be patched anymore. The boy was trying to get people to take notice of him but they were busy dragging wood for the bonfire.

A big man turned on him and shouted. The boy ran off in tears. He went behind a barn where I could see him but those working on the bonfire couldn't. He wiped his eyes on his sleeve and peered round the edge of the barn. He and I, watchers. Except he wanted their attention and I most certainly didn't.

Then he came running out waving his arms.

'Wolf! Wolf!' he cried.

This frightened me as I felt he must have seen me. In panic I wondered where to run to, when I saw him pointing in another direction to the group of men and women who had gathered around him. He was pointing beyond the barn where he had been. The group questioned him and he nodded and pointed.

Then the people went off, leaving just the boy.

So there was another wolf about I thought. What a nuisance! This was putting everyone on the alert just as they were getting over the bear hunt. In a short while people began to come back with pitch forks, hoes and shotguns.

I shivered. This was looking very dangerous.

When they group had gathered, off they went in an excited gang, waving their implements. At their head was the red-haired boy, pointing out the direction.

It was only when everyone had gone that I realised there hadn't been a wolf. I had been watching the boy all the time behind the barn. He hadn't even been looking, he was just fed up that no one was taking any notice of him. Now he had them all following him.

While everything was quiet, I took the opportunity to go downstairs and out of the barn. I drank some water that dripped out of a tap and ate a cabbage from a pile in the yard. I wandered carefully about. There was a strong smell of raw meat and someone humming. I slunk round the barn to see.

A man in a bloody apron was before a wooden table. On it was the dead bear and the man was skinning it. I shuddered in remembrance. Only that morning the bear had challenged me to hide and seek, and had then chased me into this town to seek refuge. It could easily have been me on that table with my skin half off and my guts in a heap.

I went back to my barn.

In an hour or so the people came back dejected. Their pitch forks, hoes and shotguns were no longer being waved in the air but were slung over their shoulders in a tired fashion as if they had been out working all day. I could hear the shrill voice of the boy:

'But I did see it. Honest. Honest.'

A man waved him off, and when he came back insisting on the wolf the man aimed a clip round the ear that sent the boy running off.

Chapter 13

I slept for part of that day. I couldn't get out with all the activity in the yard below me, and so there was little else to do. I had a dream which turned into a nightmare where Ma and Da, my brothers and sisters and the three little pigs were all chasing me with pitch forks, hoes and shotguns. They chased me into a house of straw. I buried my head under a cushion and could hear them all around me singing and dancing. Then the straw began to burn…

I woke with a start to the sound of music and conversation. From my window I could see the bonfire was alight, and had obviously entered my dream. The firelight lit the whole area; I could feel the heat from where I watched. All around people were sitting or standing, in brightly coloured clothes, and had mugs and plates in their hands. To one side were a group of musicians, two fiddlers, an accordion player, and a flautist, playing a lively tune.

By the side of the farm house there was a queue of people by a smaller bonfire which I couldn't see too well because they were blocking my view. When they pulled aside for an instant I was able to see the bear being roasted on a spit. A man was turning it, while a child basted it with fat and the people queued for their slice of bear meat.

All about children were running around the groups of grown-ups. One little boy I saw smacked for going too close to the fire. A girl was told off for throwing sticks in. I don't really understand human fascination with fire. It's horrid, dangerous stuff; it burns, it glares, and it throws out sparks. I've seen burnt-out cottages, barns and even a wood on fire. You would think human beings would want to keep well away from it. But there they were, having a party around it, as if it was a long lost friend.

All the activity was making it impossible for me to get away. I could hardly be in a more dangerous place. People, fire… I couldn't move from where I was until things died down.

The joke was on me. I was trapped now because I had drawn the bear towards the town. And because of that – the town was celebrating the killing of the bear. I hadn't at all meant to have him killed, but just to draw him away from me. But then I hadn't meant for Big Brother Ben to get killed either, or for Sister Sarah. In each case though I had set things going.

Was that part of the nature of being a wolf? Or the way the world treated wolves? Would I always attract killing and death because of what I was born?

How much was I to blame for that poor brute being roasted on the spit?

I consoled myself by thinking that it could have been me. All those happy people could be eating wolf meat now, as I was turned round and round over a fire with a child dripping fat over me.

I noticed the red-haired boy again; he was playing with a crowd of other children. A game had been organised for them with apples in bowls of water, and all the children ended up with wet faces. Then there were apples on strings and the children had to eat them without using their hands.

There was lots of laughter and shrieking but the apples didn't seem to come to much harm.

Then the children all got in a group, and after some arguing and shouting a girl stood in the middle blindfolded and the other children ran off. I heard the girl counting slowly.

'One, two, three…'

I almost laughed. Hide and seek! The game I and the bear had… well sort of played. And perhaps I was still playing. I watched the boys and girls finding hiding places. A boy had gone behind the musicians, a girl was crouched down at the back of a water barrel. I could see two children peering from behind a barn, another under a cart. A girl was crawling under a pile of rugs…

The sound of someone climbing my ladder brought my attention back inside. There were more serious games to play. I listened. I could hear the pad of hands and feet on the wood, and feel the shake of the floor as someone climbed. Quickly I buried myself in straw and lay as low I could.

The footsteps continued. Outside the girl still counted. 'Thirty-two, thirty-three, thirty-four…'

The footsteps stopped for an instant, then came on the loft floor and rustled the straw.

'Where shall I hide?' a boy's voice exclaimed. 'Where? Where?'

Anywhere I thought – but here.

A piece of straw was tickling my nose. I dare not move it. I wanted to sneeze, I held my breath while the boy tramped around the area, looking I presumed for the thickest patch of straw. The problem was that I had already found it.

Outside a jig was being played. The girl was still counting. 'Forty-eight, forty-nine, fifty… I'm coming!'

The boy picked up an armful of straw, and we faced each other.

It was the boy with red hair and freckles. His face had been washed and his hair slicked back, even the rip on his knee had been darned. For a long instant he stood holding the straw high, mouth wide, petrified in surprise. Our eyes seemed to have locked.

A yell from outside broke it. The boy dropped the straw, and turned about.

'Wolf! Wolf! There's a wolf!'

He went scrambling down the ladder. Quickly he dropped to the floor and ran out into the square waving his arms wildly.

'Wolf! Wolf! There's a wolf!'

I was terrified. I couldn't run out through all those people. And there was the fire too. If it came to it, I would have to be a wolf, and fight my way out. My hair bristled, I growled. I wouldn't just sit back and be taken.

I went to the window. The boy was running through everyone shouting. The music had stopped, conversation ceased, all eyes on the boy. Then he was ripped off the ground; one second he was running and in the next he was grabbed by the seat of his pants and swung over the shoulder of a large man. It was so smooth it was like part of a dance. And the next action exactly fitted. The man began smacking the boy's behind with a force that resounded through the square like a drum.

'That'll teach him!' someone shouted.

'We won't be made fools of again!'

The boy struggled and kicked. He no longer shouted wolf but just for the beating to stop. But the man went on and on, until finally a woman came to him and held his arm back. At that he laid the boy down and walked off.

For a few seconds there was silence. And then the music struck up and conversation began again. I saw the girl running around again in the renewed game of hide and seek.

But the boy lay on the ground, flat on his face, deliberately ignored by everyone.

Chapter 14

I was grateful that no one wanted to go on a wolf hunt. The boy had sent them out on a false one earlier and they didn't believe him now. Good.

I relaxed a little. The game of hide and seek was the big worry. The children could go anywhere and another might well come here. Anxiously I watched its progress. As the girl found a child they in turn became a seeker. The rules it seemed were rigid, you had to stay where you were hiding. So no one could come up here during this game, unless they cheated – and who was to say no one would?

At last they were all mopped up. Everyone found. Then a woman in a long dress had them all over and got them into pairs for dancing. Some of the children were reluctant but she was having none of that. Dance they all must. All except one who still lay face down in the dust.

The music struck up and the children danced their reel. The woman called out instructions and the children mostly knew what to do, though a couple had right and left confused. They formed two lines and danced along it in turn, then went into squares and twirled round each other. The adults watched and clapped in time to the music.

Then it was the turn of the grown-ups. Some of the children stayed to dance and some went off for food and mischief. But I was glad to see that hide and seek was no longer a choice. Glad too that everyone was busy. Dancing, clapping, eating, talking. The only problem was it looked like it might go on for a long time.

In the shadows I watched, and half wished I could dance too. Though it would have to be a dance where right and left didn't matter as I would never be able to sort them out. We wolves have music of a kind, but it's a music of misery, a group howl when we are cold and hungry. This though was for fun – and I wished I could be part of it. Instead of being hidden, I wished I could be part of them and dance for sheer joy.

A sound behind me caused me to turn. And there I saw the boy, grim-faced, coming over the top of the ladder bearing a pitchfork. He must have come up silently this time, knowing I was here, when my attention was on the music and the dancers. How could I have been so careless!

'I've got you now,' said the boy.

Of course he hadn't. A boy with a pitchfork presented no danger to me. I could easily bowl him over. The danger wasn't him, but the noise I would make. Not that the pitchfork wasn't sharp, and dangerous in the right hands. But they would need to be bigger, stronger hands.

'You got me in trouble once,' he said.

His face was sullen, there were streaks of tears. The front of his clothes were covered in dust from where he'd been lying on the ground. His hair was mussed up and he held the pitchfork before him like a spear.

Quietly I said, 'You'll only get in trouble again.'

'I've got you trapped,' he said, prodding with the pitchfork.

I was alert and watching his every move. Behind me the band struck up a lively jig.

In a way he did have me trapped. Sooner or later someone would call for him, or he could call for them. Or they would hear the noise of our struggle. Talk then, was my only weapon.

'I'm not the sort of wolf you think I am.'

The boy sneered. 'So what sort are you?'

'I'm a… good wolf.' It embarrassed me to say the last two words. Good and wolf just don't go together. And no well-brought up wolf would use the word *good* except in sarcasm. But there are times when you have to drop the niceties and say it how it is.

I got the expected reaction.

'Good wolf! There's no such thing!'

'I am,' I said. 'I've left the pack. I don't kill.'

'Don't try to fool me. I've got you trapped, and you'll lie your head off to get free.'

'I've never killed in my life,' I said.

'Don't give me that!'

'It's true.'

'Well I don't believe you.'

We stared at each other. I watched him and his pitch-fork. I watched his eyes for signs of movement, and he watched me. I knew I had to stay still and not frighten him more than he was already. It was also clear the 'good wolf' argument wasn't going to work. I had no way of proving it.

'Let me go,' I said. 'I'll be away in the morning.'

'And how many sheep will be dead?'

'None. I'll just go.'

He didn't speak for a little while. I could see he was mulling something over. I considered going for him, while his concentration wasn't quite on me. But then I had every-thing to lose if it didn't work – and I had a feeling about the boy, he didn't really know what to do – and I could work on that.

He at last said, 'I've a good mind to let you go.' After a pause, his voice rising in anger he added, 'Did you see that man belt me? I'd like to show you where his sheep are. Then when you've killed a couple, see what he says then about there being no wolf. I'd like to see his face then.'

The boy hesitated, then said, 'Would you do that?'

'Do what?'

'Kill his sheep.'

It was my turn to hesitate.

'Yes,' I at last said.

'Thought you said you didn't kill?'

I shook my head and laughed. Whatever I said was wrong. And in a way he was right. I had no intention of killing sheep. But I was willing to lie my way out of a dangerous corner.

'Look,' I said, 'You'll get more out of letting me go then turning me in.'

'How's that?' he said, suddenly remembering he was holding a pitchfork and clasping it tightly.

'If I'm a regular sort of wolf. A killer.' I said. 'And you let me go – you've everything to gain. Because I'll kill a sheep in the early morning. Then everyone will say that you were right all along…'

'They'd be sorry then.' He rubbed his backside; he was working on his bruises, inside and out.

'And if I was a *good* wolf… Well would you really want a good wolf killed and roasted on a spit?'

'I don't think they'd roast a wolf,' he said. 'They'd probably just skin you.'

'When I'm dead I hope.'

The boy grinned. I knew I was winning.

'And you also run the risk if you try to turn me in,' I said, 'of another good hiding.'

'That's true,' said the boy standing forcefully with the pitchfork, 'but suppose I stick you and shout out…'

I shook my head. 'I'm a full-size wolf. I could knock you off this platform. Of course I would probably get caught – but you'd be in hospital.'

The boy thought this one out, then said in a sudden outburst, 'Why should I do anything for them? You can eat all the sheep you like! I'm not risking another hiding.'

He dropped the pitchfork.

'Thanks,' I said.

'I don't know whether you're good or bad,' he said. 'I just know I am not going to turn you in.' He started to go down the ladder. When he was about halfway he stopped. 'Do you want some grub?'

I hadn't eaten for quite a few hours and the sight of all that eating and drinking had been rather painful. I wondered though whether I could trust the boy, but my stomach gurgled and spoke for me.

'Yes please.'

'I'll see what I can find,' he said, and disappeared down the ladder.

Chapter 15

Da had said to all of us cubs, and so many times (you know what parents are like) – 'Never trust a human being.' And here I was putting my life in the hands of one of them! Not that I had much choice with all the celebrations going on around me. I certainly couldn't go outside. That would be an embarrassingly short wolf chase. Perhaps if my leg had properly healed I could have run for it, relied on sheer speed, but a walking wolf would be a very dead wolf.

In a while I heard footsteps on the ladder. I thought of burying myself in straw but knew that would do me little good if the boy had betrayed me. I waited, alert, with no plan only fear, hearing every sound of the night. The music, the shouts, but above it all, like a drumbeat, the steps on the ladder.

The boy's head appeared. Then the rest of him, he was carrying a plate of food. I was only able to relax when he came over the top and there was clearly no one with him.

'Bear meat,' he said, putting the plate down.

My stomach turned over. I was hungry but not that hungry.

He must have seen my expression for he said, 'You really don't like meat.'

'I hate it.'

'Beautifully cooked,' he said. 'It's so juicy.'

I turned away, nauseous. 'I didn't even like him alive,' I said.

'Sorry,' said the boy and began eating the meat himself.

I watched him. He was welcome to it, tearing off bits with his greasy dirty fingers and plopping them in his mouth.

'I should've got you some cake,' he said as he chewed. 'Or just bread and butter. There's loads of fruit salad. But I just thought a wolf. Well everyone knows what wolves eat.'

I could imagine the boy by the table, walking past the cake, the bread, the fruit salad where there was no queue – and then standing in line and thinking how pleased I would be with a slab of bear meat.

'Sorry,' he said.

'Don't keep saying that.'

'Sorry... I mean –' he shook his head. 'Forget it. I'll try again later. But I've got some news...'

I pricked my ears. 'Go on.'

'There's some trouble.' He took a bite of meat and began chewing on it before he went on. 'You wouldn't believe it.' He started to laugh, then couldn't speak as the laughter took him over. He held up a hand helplessly and then began to choke. Laughter stopped, the boy spat out bits of meat and spittle, clutching at his throat. He spat some more then stayed absolutely still with just a stray moan escaping.

'Oh dear, oh dear,' he sighed. 'All that lovely meat.'

'You all right?'

'I think so.'

He took a deep breath and sank to the floor, sitting there, legs out straight breathing heavily. There were tears in his eyes. I could see he was recovering, and figured he might not welcome the obvious about eating and talking. I gave him a minute to get his breath back.

'You were saying,' I said, 'before all that – you had some news?'

He nodded. 'Wolves.'

'What?'

'That's what's so funny. Two sheep have been killed. I don't mean that's funny but it's what we were talking about. A pack of wolves has been seen…'

'I'll never get out of here,' I said.

'You'd better not try,' said the boy. 'Not now. There's a patrol out with rifles.'

'Oh great!'

'They're always worse when they've been drinking. They'll shoot at anything that moves.'

'The most stupid thing I ever did was come here,' I exclaimed.

'Well you're here,' said the boy, 'stupid or not. And you'd better stay.'

'I haven't got any choice.'

I told him about my leg.

The boy said, 'I broke mine once. Fell out of a tree. I had it in plaster for weeks.'

I wasn't too interested in the boy's tale of a broken leg. Not while there were men out there with guns hunting wolves.

He said, 'I've got to go now, they'll wonder where I am. Do you want me to come back with some grub?'

I did and I didn't. 'Someone might see you coming in here.'

'I'll take the ladder away.'

'Then how will I get down?'

'I'll put it back up when I come in the morning.'

The boy was of course right. Without a ladder no one could get up, but it also meant I was trapped here.

'Better go,' said the boy.

He began to make his way down the ladder. Just before he disappeared he stopped and his head bobbed up for an instant.'

'Sorry about the meat.'

Chapter 16

I took a look outside. There were less men about and children were being dragged off reluctantly. A couple of men came past with rifles slung over their shoulders. They certainly didn't look in party mood.

The band played on but the crowd was thinning out quickly. I suppose the news of the wolves had put a damper on things. And the bear on the spit, which I could see quite clearly now, was mostly bones. It made me feel quite peculiar; just that morning he had been throwing stones at me. It also made me decide to be careful. I must not get impatient. I must wait until things quieten down. Human beings can be awfully dangerous. And if I needed any evidence for that, I still had a back leg that wasn't quite right.

Suddenly the band stopped. I watched them packing up their instruments. No one had put any wood on the fire for a while and that was dying back to the red and charred logs that had formed the base. The remaining children were now ushered off. Pots and pans were being gathered up. A man and a woman were going round collecting rubbish.

In a little while all that was left were three people talking round the campfire. Then they went, and it was then I wished the ladder had been left. Not everything had been collected up and I could have scavenged some bits and pieces. Besides there was a dustbin left out... and there'd be some absolutely lovely stuff in that bin. Then I reflected.

Dustbin lids are noisy when you knock them off. Anyway there wasn't a ladder. I checked. So I was stuck up here with my rumbling tummy.

I pulled myself into the straw and tried to go to sleep. Not easy when you are hungry, harder still when you are surrounded by enemies. I must though have slept a little because I was woken by a man shouting:

'They had half a dozen of Charlie's chickens!'

I looked out. By the dying firelight I could see three men, all with rifles. They were talking heatedly and I caught some of the words.

'*At least six of 'em… Bob got a shot at one… Get the sheep off the high pasture… Damn wolves!*'

Then they set off in three separate directions.

Chapter 17

In the morning the boy came back. He brought me some water and party left-overs for which I was grateful. While I ate he put me in the picture.

'You can't go anywhere. Everyone's out building defences for their animals or patrolling the area.'

'I keep seeing people with guns,' I said.

'Make sure they don't see you.'

I assured him I wouldn't. I valued my skin.

'You know,' he said, 'you are a different sort of wolf.'

'And I want to stay one.'

The boy came closer and knelt down by me. He put a hand on my back. I growled at him. He quickly withdrew it.

'You don't have to do that,' he said, obviously offended.

'Sorry,' I said. 'I'm a wolf. My instinct is to bite when I get touched. It isn't you. Just what I am. I'm not a dog.'

'Does that mean we can't be friends?'

'No,' I said and meant it. 'It just means don't expect me to turn on my belly and wag my legs in the air. Go easy. Let me get to know you.'

'Sure,' said the boy. 'I don't need a pet. And...' he hesitated, 'I'm not so easy myself.'

'I've seen,' I said.

'Maybe,' he began, 'as we're both a little... well difficult... then maybe...'

He stopped. I could see he was embarrassed, shifting in his collar and I didn't feel so comfortable myself.

'Maybe,' I said.

The boy grinned. 'I'm Dan. You got a name?'

'Of course I have,' I replied, a little surprised that he thought I might not. 'Joe Wolf.'

'Pleased to meet you, Joe.'

He held out a hand. I wasn't sure what this meant, not being that well up in human customs. So I did the same and held out my paw. Dan took it and shook it. I suspected that it meant good luck so I held out my other paw. The boy didn't take that so maybe you can only have so much good luck. Pity. I needed a lot of it. But then I did have a friend, and I had never had one of those before. Maybe that was the beginning of better luck.

'How long do you think I'll have to stay up here?' I said.

Dan shrugged.

'That depends how long the wolves stay.'

Chapter 18

When the wolves had been around for a week I was sick with boredom. I had walked round and round the small area of the loft, going mad with inactivity. Every day from my window I had watched huntsmen in the square below me going off with their guns. The nights were punctured with rifle fire. Dan came each morning with food and water, and gave me the latest news.

In return I told him all about me, my life story.

'So it was you who saved Grandma!' he exclaimed. 'I read about that in the paper.'

'And it was my Big Brother Ben who got his head chopped off.'

'Well if he hadn't have messed about getting into Grandma's clothes and all that… he might have got away with it.'

'You're not sticking up for him?' I exclaimed.

'Course not. I'm just saying what a narrow squeak they had. Grandma and the girl.'

'They're lucky he was so theatrical.'

Dan agreed on that.

While I was eating my breakfast he said, 'They killed a couple of Dad's goats last night. Everyone is getting really keyed up…'

I knew that. There had been so much shooting, that it

was plain tempers were short. No way could there be that many wolves. It was obvious they weren't hitting much. There was a lot of shouting too, and arguments about who was doing what and who wasn't. Passions were getting raised, and that I found scary.

'How's your foot?' asked the boy.

'On the mend.'

'Can you run yet?'

'For a short way. I think it'll be fine in a week or two.' I sighed, 'I'm so fed up. I just want to get out of here.'

'I know,' said Dan. After a pause he added, 'I'll miss you.'

I wanted to say something comforting, he was my one friend. But what could I say? There were men out there with guns. I wasn't likely to come back.

Dan said, 'I'd hate it up here too. Cooped up. I know wolves like lots of space. But just think – it's the last place they'd look. This close to town.'

'I've got to get out. I can't stand another night.'

'You'll get shot.'

'I'll have to risk it.'

'It's getting really dangerous. Everyone is so trigger happy. The wolf pack is on the outside of town, they've got some hiding place somewhere. I don't see how you'd get away. Not with all the patrols.'

'I wish I was up to speed,' I said. 'Then…'

I could imagine myself streaking through, guns blazing after me. It was possible, just possible, that if my leg was fully healed, that I'd make it. But with a wounded back leg? Dan was right.

We didn't speak for a while. I was grateful for Dan's company and the food he brought but I was desperate to get away. This was worse than being in a zoo. There if you didn't have much space at least no one wanted to kill you.

'There's a meeting tonight so I might be a bit late,' he said. 'The Mayor's called it. Everyone to be there – except those on wolf-patrol. A strategy meeting on how to get rid of the wolves.'

'You going?'

'Yeh. Everyone is. The whole town is so angry. Nearly everyone has lost animals. People are blaming the Mayor and the Council – so he's called a meeting so we can all have our say on how to clear this area of wolves.'

'I could do it,' I said.

'Could you?'

I nodded lazily. 'Your problem is you can't find them. Well I could.'

'You sure?'

'A wolf can always find another wolf.'

The boy was silent a while then said, 'It's all very well for you to say that but my dad and my big brothers and half the town have been out there every night. And they haven't been able to get the wolves... So I don't see how you could do it.'

'I could.'

'Anyone can say that.'

'Well I could.'

'Prove it then.'

I then had a crazy idea. So crazy that I instantly rejected it first time. But then, when you are bored out of your mind, you are inclined to do some things that you might not consider in your saner moments.

'Can you get me into the Town meeting?' I said.

Chapter 19

That evening, when the sun had just gone down and there was still an orange glow in the western sky, the boy came for me. He led me down the ladder steps to the entrance of the barn where I had been virtually a prisoner for the last week.

The boy looked out carefully across the shadowy square. 'We've got to be careful,' he whispered.

I didn't need telling. I had seen the evening patrol go out, grim-faced men with rifles slung over their shoulders. To them the only good wolf was a dead one.

Dan ducked back in. An old man and woman walked hurriedly across the square.

'We'll be late,' she said.

'Don't worry,' said the old man. 'I've been to enough of these meetings in my time. It'll just be hot air to start with.'

When they had gone Dan said, 'The meeting started ten minutes ago – so there won't be many people about.'

'Except late-comers,' I said. 'And the patrols.'

'I'll go first, you stay in the shadow. When I give my whistle you come.' He demonstrated a bird whistle. I can't say what sort. The only birds I know are chickens. As Dan crossed the square I just hoped there wouldn't be a real bird of that particular variety to confuse the issue.

I waited alone, just inside the barn. A man ran across. I heard Dan talk to him. I pulled back, well inside the door.

This was a nightmare. Out there everyone was my enemy. And there was me, going to brave the dark, just to go where they all were.

Madness.

A whistle came. I hurried round the square, keeping close to the shadow of the buildings. Night was dropping fast, the quicker the better. I saw Dan by a group of trees. I hurried to him, as lightfooted as I could, and then laid myself down flat close to the foot of a large tree.

Dan pointed out where we were going next. He then set off, and had hardly gone twenty metres when two huntsmen came from behind a building walking towards him.

'Hi,' he called.

'Aren't you going to the meeting?' said one of them.

'Soon,' said Dan.

'Waste of time,' said the other.

I lay utterly motionless while they continued on their way, discussing whether the meeting we were going to had any point to it. Dan watched them until they disappeared and then went on in the direction they had come. In a minute or so he whistled and I followed after.

It seemed an awful long way to the meeting hall, but then, as Dan said, we couldn't go the direct way. Well we went, I am sure, the most indirect way. From time to time there was shooting, mostly at a distance, but once close enough to make my blood freeze.

Dan met hunters every so often. He greeted them cheerfully. He met also late-comers and a few people who just weren't going to the meeting; people who had already made their minds up or people who thought no one would listen to them. Dan said hello to them all as if he was just playing out.

So far Dan had met them all.

I was crossing an open area between two barns when it was my turn. Two hunters came out from the side of a barn. I was well in the open. I froze, it was almost dark now, and I could see them better then they could see me. Wolves have good night vision. I also knew it was pointless me trying to run. I hoped that in the darkness they might miss me. That was a short-lived thought.

'What's that?' said one of the men.

'Where?'

'There.' He pointed.

They came towards me peering through the gloom. I looked around for the best place to run. This whole scheme was stupid. My impatience was going to get me shot. One of the men put a rifle to his shoulder… I braced myself. I would have to run.

He took aim…

Then there came a call and clap of the hands.

'Hey Rover – this way!'

It was Dan at right-angles to the men. I scampered across, looking as dog-like as I could. I even licked his hand.

'You'd better put that dog in,' one of the man called. 'I nearly shot him.'

'Sorry.'

'Don't be sorry. Lock him up.'

The men went on their way. And in a few minutes so did we.

Chapter 20

'I'll go in,' said Dan. 'You stay out here till I call you.' I was on a sandbox, just below a window by the side of the meeting hall. It wasn't much of a hall, just a large wooden hut with windows all round and a door at the front. The wood was brown board, cracked and stained. It probably leaked in wet weather.

The window near me was slightly open, and if I kept to the side I could see what was going on without being seen.

The hall was packed and noisy.

I wanted Dan to stay. I needed his protection; outside a hall of human beings and with gunmen wandering about. But I couldn't keep him – so I feebly waved a paw as he left me to go round the front and in the door.

I tried to settle down. I needed to know what was going on in the meeting. From where I lay I had a clear view of the Mayor. He was sitting alone on a low platform facing the audience. There was table in front of him but the only thing on it was his gavel and plate. He had a bright red face, and sleeked black hair which shone in the electric light. Around his neck was his chain of office hanging in a half-circle of gold.

The meeting was rowdy. The Mayor's eyes flickered, the muscles in his face twitched as he tried to watch everyone and defend himself at the same time. Then he bashed his little hammer with fervour, shouting out, 'Order! Order!'

A man I couldn't see was making a suggestion:

'We could dig a deep pit, and put some sheep in it. Then the wolves would jump in, kill the sheep, stuff themselves and won't be able to get out!'

Someone offered the man a shovel so long as he used his own sheep. Personally I felt sorry for the animals.

'Order! Order!' yelled the Mayor. 'If you have a suggestion put up your hand. Don't shout out. Yes Mrs. Guthrie?'

Mrs. Guthrie's thoughts had obviously been triggered by the last speaker. She suggested a lot of deep holes with spikes in, and then covered with a thin layer of sticks and soil.

'When a wolf walks over,' she exclaimed, 'It'll fall through.'

'Wolf kebab!' shouted someone.

A very reasonable woman in the front said, 'Suppose a child fell through?'

Mrs. Guthrie said everyone would be given maps showing where the holes were.

The woman said, 'I'm a teacher and half my pupils can't read maps.'

The Mayor banged his gavel to stop the laughter and comments. I heard someone say it was one way of getting rid of less able pupils. And I wondered about Mrs. Guthrie – how did she treat her own kids, if she had any? Did she have spikes in her larder in case they got peckish in the night?

A man in the middle stood and showed the audience a mousetrap. I had to strain to hear him over the jeers.

'If we built one a metre long,' he shouted. 'With a strong enough spring and baited it with mutton chops…'

The town blacksmith told the man that a metre-long mouse trap would have a spring too strong for anyone to bait. Someone else told him that it would be full of cats and dogs.

A woman suggested poison gas.

A man asked her if she knew how much gas masks cost. She didn't. The man went on to say that the County would have to buy one for everyone and force them to wear it all the time... He then suggested gas masks for sheep and cattle too, but the woman had already sat down defeated.

There were quite a few more suggestions but they all had something wrong with them. For instance:

'*Drowning the wolves.*'

'*Freezing them.*'

'*Starving them.*'

'*Driving them out with lots of noise.*'

'*Painting the wolves with luminous paint.*'

At this last suggestion one wag shouted, 'Why not put bells round their necks!'

'*Bring in bears to chase them off.*'

'*Wolf fleas.*'

Here it was noted that most wolves already had them. And I could vouch for that. One of the few advantages of being a lone wolf is that you don't catch anyone else's fleas.

'*Beer in the drinking water.*'

The Mayor misheard and thought the person said 'bear' which might have been an improvement.

'*Shut all our animals up for six months.*'

'*A three-metre fence round the County.*'

The man looked rather shame-faced when it was pointed out that the wolves were already *in* the County.

'*Try to make friends with them.*'

I rather liked this one. It wouldn't work but it was much nicer than spikes in holes. I suppose it was a suggestion out of desperation because by this time the suggestions had stopped. Either there were no new ones or people were just recycling the old. At one point the meeting got very bad-tempered. One man had a long go at the Mayor and said he should resign immediately and hold an election.

The Mayor said, 'Suppose I do resign, Mr. Smith, and you became Mayor… How would *you* get rid of the wolves?'

Unfortunately this was the man who favoured the giant mouse-trap. An election was not thought to be a good idea. Judging by the audience it is not likely he would have got many votes.

It was then Dan stood up on a chair. He called out but couldn't be heard in all the chatter and banter. He looked very small in that great crowd of people, their arms waving like a heaving sea. From his expression I could tell he was quite afraid, and at this point, in my own nervousness, I would not have minded if he had thought better of it. I didn't like the audience and was fearful how they might react.

'Order! Order' shouted the Mayor banging on his plate with the gavel. 'One of our younger citizens has a suggestion. Please give him the courtesy of listening.'

'Has he seen another wolf?' someone shouted.

This brought added laughter. The Mayor shouted for order, and conversation died to an eager buzz. Dan waited.

'Get on with it,' shouted a man.

Dan ignored him. I was very impressed. I could see the courage growing in him. Finally when there was not a sound to be heard he said:

'I know someone who can rid this town of wolves.'

There was uproar at this. From all over the hall comments were shouted in a cacophony of ridicule and anger.

'Order! Order!'

The Mayor had to hammer repeatedly to get the audience quiet enough so he could ask the obvious question.

'Who, young man? Who?'

'He's outside, your Worship.'

That quietened everyone. They couldn't understand why someone with so bold a claim wasn't inside.

'Bring him in,' said the Mayor.

Chapter 21

I came into the hall and the meeting went wild. Men shouted and screamed, women fainted. I was kicked and buffeted as I made my way down the aisle with Dan alongside. It was the most terrifying walk of my life. I had to endure their murderous hate, even though my heart was beating like a grandfather clock and my legs trembling so much they could hardly support me. It was a gauntlet of arms, legs and insults.

When I got to the front the furore did not stop. I knew that human beings hated wolves but I had never been amongst so many. If I had I realised I would never have dared to come. But now, out in front of them, my way to the door blocked, I saw the madness of my position.

I had simply walked into the enemy thinking I could persuade them. Far easier to persuade the wind not to blow.

The Mayor let the audience rage. There was little he could do to stop them. He could bang his gavel until the end of the World and it would have had no effect.

I wondered whether I would get any hearing at all.

Dan bent low and tried to say something to me. I couldn't make out a word. It hardly mattered; the chances of me getting out of the hall alive were low. It was the most stupid thing I had ever done, coming here; a wolf believing he would be welcomed by a town who were terrorised by wolves!

It would be a crazy person indeed who would bet on my future.

As if to point this out the Meeting Hall door opened and through it came a man with a rifle. Heads turned to him, and the crowd gradually quietened as they all became aware of his presence. For a little while he stood framed in the door, the gun gripped in his hands where it was swung, and pointed at me.

He began to walk down the aisle. His eyes were steely blue, the light reflecting in them as they gazed unflinching at me. His jaw was tight and determined, with no suggestion of mercy. The crowd were hushed. The man licked his lips…

My only chance was to rush in amongst the legs and chairs. It would not be much of a chance. I still had to get to the door, through a crowd where everyone was hostile. I might snap a few bones but in the end I would be shot like a mad dog.

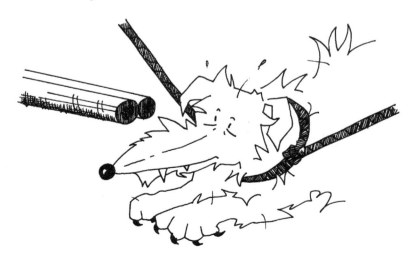

I watched the man's fingers. As soon as I sensed movement I would dart in amongst the chairs. My attention was distracted as a rope was thrown over my head. And then quickly another one, and I suddenly found myself being drawn in two directions by the neck. I was choking and helpless as the man with the rifle strode in on me.

The hall was quiet apart from the pleading of Dan.

'Please, Mr Mayor – he has come to help us. Please everyone. Listen! Please!'

The Mayor banged his gavel. 'Order! Order!'

The room hushed. The two ropes round my neck were pulled tight by the two stout men who strained across me. The man with the gun was standing over me, the barrel inches from my face. I could see into its darkness a short way. Not far enough to make out the bullet but I had no hope the gun was not loaded. Besides which the man had a beltful.

The Mayor turned to Dan.

'This is a dreadful insult to the people of this County. Why have you done it?'

'Please, sir…' Dan was trembling so much, he could barely get his words out. 'He's come to help us. This wolf is… my friend.'

A shocked gasp came from the audience.

'Some friends you have, young man,' said the Mayor sternly.

'He should be shot with the wolf!' someone yelled.

The Mayor banged his gavel. 'This is a civilised County! We do not execute children. Even children who plainly do not know right from wrong.'

'He's my friend,' exclaimed Dan. He made a wild appeal to the audience. 'He's a good wolf.'

The audience gasped in horror and from its midst came cries:

'Shoot the wolf!'

'Hang him up on a fence!'

'Skin him and flog the boy!'

'Shoot him!'

The last cry grew until everyone was shouting it in dreadful chorus.

'Shoot him! Shoot him! Shoot him!'

I knew that was the end. The ropes were pulled tighter about my neck, and the gun barrel aimed between my eyes.

Dan climbed up on the Mayor's table. He was facing a wild and furious sea that would smash anything in its way.

'He saved Grandma!' he yelled above the wind and waves. 'He's a good wolf!'

'Shoot him! Shoot him! Shoot him!'

The Mayor nodded to the man with the gun. Insanely I wondered whether I would have time to hear the bang. Dan was still shouting. I tried to hear only his words, the last words I would hear on Earth.

'He saved Grandma! He's a good wolf!'

It was then a blonde-haired man walked into the aisle. I hadn't noticed him before in the packed audience. He was tall and wore leather trousers with an axe hanging from his belt.

'Stop! I know this wolf!'

Chapter 22

The man told his story to the stunned audience. He said at first he had not recognised me. One wolf looks much like another he said (at some other time I might have argued this point) – and it was only when he had heard Dan say I had saved Grandma that he realised who I was.

Luckily for me the woodcutter happened to be visiting his mother who lived locally, and he'd also brought along his daughter.

She stepped out of the audience. It was the little girl in the red cloak and hood who I had met in the woods. She walked forward and threw her arms round my neck.

'Oh wolf!' she said, 'we owe you everything.'

My muzzle was washed by her tears or were they my own? The ropes all at once relaxed round my neck, and when I next looked the barrel of the gun was pointing at the floor and the man holding it was smiling at me.

Then I must admit I wept. For the first time I knew I was going to get out of the hall alive.

The audience all at once swept over to my side. A big factor must have been the sight of me with the girl in red with her arms round my neck. I reminded them of the family dog.

'This alters everything,' said the Mayor. He turned to me. 'I must apologise on behalf of this county for our lack of manners.'

There were mumbles of 'hear hear' from the audience.

'I understand,' I said, though I thought that ropes round my neck and a gun barrel in my face went beyond the realms of bad manners. Better though to accept the goodwill I was now getting than argue it into something worse.

The woodcutter lifted off the ropes that were still hanging limply round my neck. I looked over that sea of expectant faces and was unsure I had any words left. My throat was dry. One minute at death's door and then the conquering hero – and now expected to make my case for ridding the town of wolves... My thoughts could not move so quickly.

Dan came over and whispered, 'They are with you now. There won't be a better time.'

I realised he was right. I could see from their faces they were sorry for the way they had treated me, and they would do almost anything I wanted. I only had to ask.

I made my way round the Mayor's table and supported myself on it by my front legs facing the audience. My practice at walking upright had at last come in useful. The hall was quiet, waiting for me. How different from ten minutes before when they were baying for my blood.

I told them about myself. It was a simple way to begin while I cleared my head over more complicated matters. I told them how I had been kicked out by my family because I would not kill. I told them how I had saved the three little pigs. While I was telling this I suddenly realised that these people ate pig. Might they not think me stupid for defending an animal they butchered for Sunday lunch?

But strangely they liked what I had to say. I could see their faces dropping into soft smiles as I went through the story. I rather think it was because the pigs wore clothes and lived in houses. They weren't the sort of pigs you ate with beans and egg.

They made exceptions of them. Well wasn't that what I wanted from them? To persuade them that I was not the regular sort of wolf. The sort that you shot on sight.

I ended my tale by telling them how I had had to leave the three little pigs. I hoped they would recognise the parallel. The pigs had asked me to leave not because of what I was but because of what other wolves were. Exactly the same applied in this meeting room. I was asking them to see me for what I was – not what they thought me to be.

I stopped. There was no point telling them about my time in their County. That had nothing to add, and might make them forget the point I wanted to make. And I had run out of words. I was suddenly very tired.

The Mayor said, 'Thank you for that, Joe Wolf.'

The woodcutter began to clap, then Dan and the girl in red. The audience joined in. I could not believe how they had changed. The man with the gun had put it down and was clapping too. My face was streaked with tears. It was not just from happiness but from sheer relief.

When the applause had ceased the Mayor said, 'You say you can get rid of the wolves, Joe?'

'Yes, I can.'

'How?'

I addressed the audience. 'I can hunt them down. I can track them. I can smell them. I know where a wolf goes. Instead of your hunters going everywhere – under my guidance they would go straight to where the wolf pack is.'

The Mayor said thoughtfully, 'I can see that.'

The woodcutter said, 'We've nothing to lose.'

'The County must decide,' said the Mayor, stiffening and becoming an official again. 'All those in favour of us accepting the help of Joe Wolf – say aye.'

'Aye!' came a great chorus.

'Those against say no.'

There was not a sound.

'The ayes win!' exclaimed the Mayor.

Cheering filled the hall. And went on and on.

I had won them over.

The Mayor came round to me. He held up his hands for silence and when at last he had it he said, 'Joe Wolf, do you agree to be sheriff of this county?'

'I do.'

'Hold up your right paw.'

I wasn't sure which one it was but made a lucky guess.

'Do you swear, Joe Wolf, to uphold the honour of the sheriff's office?'

'I do.'

'Do you swear, Joe Wolf, to do your utmost to uphold the highest standards of law and order in order to protect the citizens of this county?'

'I do.'

'Then with the authority invested in me, I appoint you sheriff...'

The rest was lost in cheers.

Chapter 23

The meeting agreed that I should take over the sheriff's office. Six deputies were appointed, one of whom was the woodcutter. I said I wanted a seventh. The Mayor said that was agreeable and I indicated Dan.

When the Mayor looked a little uncomfortable at this, I reminded him that Dan had brought me here in the first place.

'Give him a go!' shouted someone.

'Yeh, it'll straighten him out.'

The Mayor saw it was the mood of the meeting and so swore Dan in. There was no one more proud than Dan when he was sworn in by the Mayor.

The meeting broke up.

I was accompanied to my new office by Dan, the little girl, and the woodcutter. Behind us came the townsfolk. Everyone agreed it would be safer. They didn't want their new sheriff shot by one of the patrols who did not yet know that I was a different sort of wolf.

It was a cheery procession. The bubble of sound behind felt good and reassuring. And here I was, walking with the woodcutter, the little girl and Dan. For the first time in my life I felt wanted.

I was the sheriff.

My office was a stout wooden building. Only Dan came in, he was going to stay the night. He said he'd always wanted to sleep in the sheriff's office. Coming in off the street we came into the main office. It had a big desk, chairs, filing cabinets, cupboards and a hat rack.

'This is a real office!' exclaimed Dan. We were both impressed by the hat rack.

I tried out various of the chairs but there was no hurry in fixing on one.

At one end of the office was a cell with bars from floor to ceiling. Its only furniture was a bed. Through a door there was a small bedroom, with a bed, cupboard, shelves and so forth. I decided that Dan could sleep there. I would sleep on a mat in the office. I'd be far more comfortable.

Dan said, 'I want to sleep in the cell.'

'OK,' I said. There was no one else using it. And why not enjoy ourselves? Soon enough we'd have to get on with the job in hand.

Chapter 24

When I woke in the morning for a few seconds I didn't know where I was. I saw a room, with strange furniture and the sun shining through the window. My first thoughts were those of panic. What was I doing in a human house!

Then the sight of the desk, the filing cabinet and the hat rack reminded where I was, and all that had happened last night. I lifted my head and saw across to the cell. Through the bars I could see Dan asleep on the bed, most of the blankets on the floor.

I should have felt happy. Pleased with my performance, pleased I had somewhere to live and a job. Pleased that I was at last somebody. But it all felt very shaky. What has been given can be taken away. I had seen how the audience wanted to string me up one minute and were eating out my hand the next. They were fickle and could easily switch back.

I had made promises. I had said of course I can get rid of the wolves. Maybe Dan was right – anyone can say that. Doing it was something else.

I had been appointed sheriff. Was I really? I didn't feel like it this morning. I felt like a wolf, a wolf wondering what he was doing in this place surrounded by human beings. Wondering how I could feel more like a sheriff.

I got up and shuffled around. I needed some fresh air, perhaps that might break up these tired thoughts of mine.

The door had been left on the latch, I pushed it and went out. The bright sunlight quite overpowered me. I blinked to get used to the whiteness. I took a deep breath and then wished I hadn't; it was full of street dust.

'Morning Sheriff,' said a young man walking past with a bag of tools. He stopped. 'Great meeting last night.'

'It had its moments,' I said.

'You can say that again!' He chuckled. 'I feel sorry for the wolves…' Then caught himself. 'I didn't mean you. I meant *those* wolves.'

'I know what you mean.'

'No offence,' said the young man, 'but we've never had a wolf as a sheriff in this town before. Well we've never had a wolf as *anything* in this town. No, let me start again…' He took a breath then continued. 'We've never had a wolf in this town before. Never, ever. And it is going to take some getting used to. It's all right with the young people, but some of the old ones… Well you know what old folks are. They think it'll never work out.'

'They're wrong,' I said.

'That's what I tell 'em. And the sooner you get rid of them wolves, the sooner they'll believe it.'

'They'll be gone tonight,' I said.

'You sure act fast, Sheriff. Must be on my way. Good luck!' And he headed along.

I stayed outside a little longer. A few passers-by greeted me and I gave them my confident view of the world. When I had done it three times I felt that was enough. It was a bit like lying. I turned to go back in and saw a cardboard box by the door. It was full of vegetables, cereals and things. It hadn't been there last night, so I guessed it must be for me.

Someone was being thoughtful.

I dragged the box in.

Everyone was being nice. But that was because they expected something of me. Results! It was all very well me acting brash and confident, just because I was sheriff and had an office with a cell in it. That might fool some people but it didn't fool me, no more than it would fool the wolves.

I began to think about this. About why I was being treated differently... All the 'Morning, Sheriff' stuff. I wasn't complaining about that. But how deep did it go? So much of the way people treat you is because of what you look like. The farmer shot at me because he saw a wolf. Suddenly I felt a cold grip on my heart. Why should they stop shooting at me? I didn't mean intentionally, but at night say. There I am, out hunting wolves, doing my job. A patrol man sees the shadowy outline of a wolf in the trees. He's not going to shout, 'Is that you, Sheriff?' He's just going to shoot.

Would I be a dead sheriff or just another dead wolf?

Dan was getting up. He stretched. 'That bed's hard.'

'Better not take up a life of crime then.'

He laughed as he put his clothes on. 'What's it feel like being sheriff?'

'I don't look like a sheriff,' I said.

'That's because you haven't got the uniform.'

'What uniform?'

Dan went to a large cupboard and opened it. 'Here.'

I came over. The cupboard was full of clothes and gear.

'Try this,' said Dan. He held out a waistcoat with a silver star on it.

'How I am suppose to get that on?'

'You've got to stand up,' said Dan.

I did so. Dan came behind me and put my front legs

through the holes. Then he came round and did the buttons up.

'Smart,' he said.

I strutted about, my paws tucked under my armpits.

'Now you're at least half a sheriff,' said Dan.

'Mind your manners, deputy' I said turning eagerly back to the cupboard.

Dan handed me a cowboy hat. 'You must have one of these.'

I put it on.

'Not bad.' Dan twisted back and forth looking me over. 'You need some slits for your ears.'

He took it off me and went over to the desk. There in a drawer he found some scissors and a piece of chalk. He came back, put the hat on me and marked with chalk where my ears were.

'I should be a tailor,' he said, taking the hat off, and going to work on it with the scissors.

I put on a pair of jeans. They were too long.

'I'll do them next,' he said.

Over the morning we worked on my gear. The hat was fine, the ear-holes helped to keep it on. Dan cut down the jeans. There was a pair of high boots in the cupboard. They looked really slick but when I tried them on they were just totally wrong for my feet. I took them off.

'Useless.'

Dan insisted. 'You've got to have boots.'

'I've got paws. These are made for human feet.'

We tried stuffing them with rags and newspaper. That didn't work. Then Dan had his idea.

'We'll take the bottom of the heel off.'

I didn't understand at first. So Dan showed me. It

seemed pretty odd. My feet would poke through the boots.

'Then they won't be boots,' I said.

'So what? They're just for show.'

About midday I put everything on. The waistcoat and star, the cowboy hat, the jeans and the boots (with my feet poking out like castors).

Dan looked me over.

'What do you think?'

'Almost there,' he said. 'Just something missing.'

Dan went to a drawer at the bottom of the cupboard. He searched about and came out with a gunbelt complete with two holsters and two six-guns.

'I'm not wearing that,' I said. 'Too many of my family have been shot.'

Dan said, 'They're fake. Like your boots. Just for show.'

'I don't know,' I said. 'Ma and Da hate guns.'

'Real guns,' said Dan.

'The idea of guns.'

'Well just try it on,' said Dan.

I put on the gunbelt, and found it gave me extra weight low down. Walking with it was a lot easier than walking without it.

'Think of them as ballast,' said Dan.

I walked around the office. I tried to draw a gun. I couldn't, and thought it was my paw that couldn't get a grip. Then I saw Dan grinning.

'I said they were fake,' he said.

'They're stuck in the holster!' I exclaimed.

''Fraid so, Sheriff.'

'Suits me,' I said.

I blew on my star and polished it up. And suddenly felt like a real sheriff.

'Let's go for a walk,' said Dan.

Chapter 25

We went out into the street. Dan wore his deputy badge and a waistcoat over his everyday clothes. I wore the works; cowboy hat, waistcoat, jeans, high boots and gunbelt complete with guns. I wanted the town to know they had a sheriff.

We walked the main street. Our intention was to go up one side and back down the other. Sheriff and Deputy walked slow and steady, side by side. We were the law, and criminals had better watch out. They weren't to know my six-guns were fake. I rather hoped there would be no crime today. It would be humiliating to have to get down on all fours to chase someone.

My boots had a tendency to jog up and down against my legs. And even with the added weight of the six-guns it was a lengthy walk.

'Morning, Sheriff' had changed to 'Afternoon, Sheriff.'

I smiled at people or held up a paw. I would have liked to have raised my hat but it was stuck too firmly over my ears. Passers-by remarked on the weather. I told them it was 'very pleasant' and 'yes, I was enjoying their town'. A woman introduced her son to me, and told me to have a good look at him. The boy poked out his tongue behind his mother's back. While I distracted her Dan made vile threats to the boy.

A couple of old people made comments on 'kids today' and I agreed 'parents were too soft.'

As we passed the newspaper office a man with a green eyeshield ran out.

'Sheriff! A photo please.'

Dan and I posed. I picked my teeth with a match so I could look really mean. Dan scowled too. The photographer tried to soften our pose by asking us to say cheese and such-like. But we were having none of it. This wasn't a wedding picture.

A small crowd had gathered. The photographer asked them to step back and would I pose with guns pointed.

I told him I would only get my guns out to use.

The crowd approved.

'Enough photos,' I said. Dan and I crossed the street.

My forelegs were beginning to ache. I felt I had to hold them over my six-guns, as if ever ready to draw. My boots, which had my feet poking out the bottom, were rubbing up and down on the fur of my shins. What we do to look good!

By the time we got back to the office I was hobbling.

'They were really impressed,' said Dan.

'Get me a bowl of water, Deputy!'

'That badge makes you really bossy.'

I soaked my feet and shins while Dan sorted me out a pair of socks.

'That's enough public relations,' I said as I rubbed my feet. 'I've got some wolves to sort out. Let's have all the deputies here in one hour.'

Chapter 26

We set off as soon as the sun had gone down, eight of us in single file. There was me, Dan, the woodcutter and the other five deputies. All had rifles except Dan and myself.

The lead was taken by Dan. He had persuaded me to let him. He knew the way about he said, hadn't he been running around the town and surrounding fields and woods since he could walk? I thought he was exaggerating but I knew how keen he was. He didn't want to be thought of forever as 'that silly kid who cried wolf'.

Having him in the lead would also keep him out of mischief.

We started from the sheriff's office and walked out of town. Once clear of buildings we made our way across the fields to the farms on the outskirts. By this time it was dark, the night clear and moonless. A glory of stars shone overhead once we were free of the town lights.

I was wearing my sheriff's gear. Well I didn't want to be accidentally shot. The uniform also had authority and I wanted it clear I was in charge. There was only one sheriff on this trip, only one plan. Besides which, guns are dangerous. I didn't want wild shooting. That would only scare off the wolves, and waste our evening. Any shooting had to be on target.

I wore socks to keep my boots from chafing and carried

a stout stick as added support. It also occurred to me, that with my useless six-guns, the stick might prove my only useful weapon. I was glad it was dark. It didn't quite suit my image being a sheriff with a stick, not to mention having guns stuck fast in my holster.

Having got out of town, our plan was simply to visit three outlying farms. I had sent word ahead that they were to leave animals out in certain fields. Other farms had been told to bring theirs in. We had no particular order as we had no idea where the wolves would be. The evening attacks had no pattern.

Several things could happen. We might miss the wolves, we might scare the wolves, or we might find them… I no longer had my confidence of the daylight. There was too much space out here and too much I just couldn't plan.

I ordered no talking. Two deputies who were smoking were told to put out their cigarettes and not light up again. While we walked we had to be as quiet as possible, when we stopped we must stop in silence. Otherwise the wolves would hear us and be off.

Our most important asset was surprise.

We skirted a hill farm where sheep were grazing. Once we had found the sheep we backed off and waited by some rocks. Here we had coffee and sat it out for an hour. Then we decided to try another farm.

As we came closer I smelt wolf.

I stopped the team and gave my last orders. They were up ahead, downwind of us. The deputies were to go no further. I would go on ahead and they must await my signal.

Chapter 27

I went a short way, until my deputies were out of sight. Then I took off my gear. I folded the waistcoat with its sheriff's badge and the jeans. I put the cowboy hat, the high boots, and the gun holsters with their guns on top of the other clothing and put them all under a hedge. I placed the stick with them and had an instant's worry about whether I might be able to find it all again. But then I thought so what if I couldn't. I had a cupboard full of clothes.

I dropped onto four legs and made my way stealthily into the field. It was on a hill, I on one side, making my way up the slope, and the wolves somewhere down the other. I could smell them strongly as the breeze blew towards me. It was unlikely they could smell me, and anyway why should they worry? My scent was faint compared to theirs, and a lone wolf was small danger to a pack.

A little closer, I could smell a fresh kill. The odour of warm blood almost hissed in the air and made me feel safer. Wolves round a kill have little thought for anything else. They are too eager, fighting for the best bits.

Then I could hear them. A low growling, as they pushed and pulled each other, competing for the meat. Though the night had hushed them somewhat, and they made an attempt to keep the racket down – every so often a snarl cut the air.

From the top of the hill I could just make them out. Below me, shadows going to and fro, panting, growling, the weaker ones being pushed away from the prey and having to wait. I inched towards them, the turf cold underfoot, a dew settling.

As I came gingerly in on them, I tried to make out the numbers. Five, no six, perhaps seven as they moved over and around, in and out of each other for bits of the kill. The dead animal was probably a sheep, this was grazing land. I hoped it was a plump one; eating it would make them heavy and sluggish.

My plan was simple enough. I had no wish for wolves to be killed. I was going to go in and warn them of the danger they were in. I hoped that they might listen to another wolf.

I stopped fifty metres away and let them eat some more. I tried to renew my courage. I had told the town I could get rid of the wolves. Well there they were, six or seven jaws tearing at a carcass. Could I?

Two wolves were scrapping, and I was close enough to hear them. It was funny to watch. It sounded just like my family at dinner.

'That's mine!'

'Well it isn't now!'

'Give it back!'

'Make me!'

'I said hand over, dog-face!'

Another, older voice, broke in. 'Stop squabbling. Do you want to get us shot!'

It was… it couldn't be. Leader of the pack. The one who tried to make me kill. The one who had thrown me out. The one whom I had shamed. It couldn't be.

A cry escaped from me. 'Da!'

'Who's that?'

I made my way towards them, unsure of anything.

'Who are you?' called Da.

It was too dark to make him out amongst the other wolves. They had given up eating and were facing me. Then Da stepped forward from the group, he turned to the rest.

'Stay.'

Da continued towards me, a slow, wary walk. Two metres away he stopped. Da sniffed, paused, sniffed again.

'Joe?'

'It's me.'

'What you doing here?'

I didn't answer. He was my Da. I always said the wrong things to him.

Da sniffed again. 'I can smell people about you. You been with them?'

'Yes.'

'You always were a weird wolf.'

'I'm sheriff here.'

'Well I don't know what that is – but it sounds good.' He turned to the rest of the pack. 'It's Joe! He's a… what did you say?'

'Sheriff.'

'*Joe – the veggie?*'

'*He's a what?*'

'*What's he doing here?*'

The pack shuffled closer, eager to hear what we had to say.

'So why have you come, boy?'

'To warn you.'

'Of what?'

'If you stay you'll be shot,' I said.

The pack growled. I could feel them bristling, ready.

'They won't find us,' said Da.

'I did.'

He was silent, watching me, coming no closer but trying to search me out.

At last he said, 'Would you bring humans after us?'

'If you stay.'

The pack growled and edged in closer, to come into a line with Da, as if there was a fence they wouldn't yet cross. I could feel their warm breath and smell the meat they had just eaten.

'You're braver than I thought,' said Da, 'but stupider too.'

'I don't want any of you killed,' I said trying to hide my fear.

'None of *us* will be,' came a growl from the pack.

There was nothing I could do but hold my stand. My deputies were too far away. And if I tried to run they would rip me to bits like the sheep they had been eating.

'You've got a nerve,' said Da. 'Coming here, coming from the enemy.'

'I came to warn you.'

'You used to be a wolf,' he said. 'But now you're one of *them*.'

I was thrown back as a wolf from the line sprang forward and pounced on me. I crashed on the ground and the wolf jumped on me. Our jaws clashed and grappled, our paws fought and pushed. I was in terror that the others would come in to help as we bit and rolled. In a flurry we snapped, and whipped about each other. I closed my jaw round flesh, feeling a crunch of bone and a flow of blood…

'Enough!' yelled Da.

He came between us and pushed us apart, the way he

used to when I was a cub. He cuffed my opponent round his ear.

'We don't kill our own,' snarled Da.

'That traitor!' hissed the other wolf.

'Not our own!' exclaimed Da. 'We kill for food.'

The pack growled resentfully.

I tipped back my head and howled into the night, two long howls. I ignored them all, and dared them to do as they wished as I made my cry, the call of the wolf. But I was not calling to wolves; this was my signal to my deputies: the strategy I had prepared in advance. There followed a barrage of rifle shot as they fired their warning into the sky. The sounds pierced the night like trees crashing in the forest. Even though they were from my friends the shots made me tremble with the other wolves. They were the sounds of our nightmares.

'They'll kill us!' shrieked one of the pack.

'Not tonight,' I said.

'But tomorrow…?' asked Da. He too was shivering.

'Go,' I said. 'Please.'

Da gave himself a shake as if he'd just had a soaking, He struggled for words. 'You and them… would come for us, with guns?'

'You threw me out,' I said.

'Was I not right?'

The pack growled their agreement.

'Where could I go?' I appealed. 'Where? When every wolf was hostile?'

'Anywhere,' he said, 'Anywhere but with… them.'

'How would you know what it's like?' I said. 'You've always lived amongst wolves. Never been out of the pack… How would you know?'

'I know it was hard…' he said uncomfortably. 'But did you have to go to human beings?'

'Da…' I began and stopped. I could never make him understand that friendship had been offered and I had to take it. The rules were different. I was different.

We did not speak for a while, silenced by our love and hate. Neither of us wanted to argue. Time was short, and who knew when we would meet again?

'Me and your Ma,' he said at last, 'we wondered how you were making out.'

'Has she had the new litter?'

'Six of 'em. Three of each. All guzzling like nobody's business.'

'Tell her…' What did I want to tell her? I could hardly think. 'Tell her I'm sorry I couldn't be what she wanted.'

'She knows.' He looked about him and sniffed the air. 'Which way is safe?'

'That way.' I pointed in a direction away from my deputies.

He turned to the pack. 'There's plenty of other places to hunt.'

The wolves growled resentfully, still frightened, confused.

'Look after yourself, boy.'

'And you.'

Da gazed at me for a second or two as if there was something he still wanted to say. Then shrugged as if it was too difficult to put into words. He began walking away, followed by the others.

I watched them padding across the soft turf, closely behind each other, wolf after wolf. Once Da turned and looked back. I had that same feeling he wanted to say something, but he turned back and in a few seconds the pack merged into the darkness.

I stayed a while longer, trying to make them out in the cave of the night. But they had gone.

Really gone.

Chapter 28

Joe said I could write this last chapter. Me, Dan. He said I could finish the story.

He told me he'd said all he'd wanted to say. He had done what he promised to do – and what more was there to write? I said people would want to be brought up to date. He said well you do it then. So this is me writing. I don't write as well as Joe. I just have to do it how I speak. So bear that in mind when you're reading.

What I actually think is that Joe was tired out by all the writing. It's an awful lot of pages, nearly a whole book of it, and its not easy hitting a keyboard with paws. Also I think he was upset at the end of the last chapter – you know with his Da going and all that. And Joe not knowing whether he would ever see him again. That would be bound to affect you.

Mind you, if it was me, I'd be all right again after a couple of weeks, then I'd get on and write this chapter. So just in case that might happen to Joe, I'd better get it done. You see, I do have a few things to say myself.

Before I could begin writing I had to read what he wrote, and mostly I agree with it, except some of the bits he wrote about me; I wouldn't have said them in quite the same way. I did try to get him to change a few bits but he wouldn't. I don't think that's quite fair – but it makes it even more important that I write this chapter.

Sort of to get even.

Lets get back to the wolves. Like Joe said, they had gone. Of course it took a while for the town to accept that. That's only reasonable. They hardly knew Joe and just because he says they're gone doesn't mean they are. You really have to know for certain about some things. Like wolves, especially if you keep sheep or chickens.

So for a time people kept saying to each other 'none last night'. They were out still guarding their property just in case. But after a while they stopped saying 'none last night' and then a bit later they stopped going out and guarding. Then it became obvious to everyone that the wolves really had gone.

Joe had done what he promised.

After that he was made permanent sheriff instead of temporary. But really the most important thing to come out of that whole episode was the meeting me and the woodcutter called of the deputies. That was just before he, the woodcutter not Joe, had to go back home with his daughter, Little Red Riding Hood (odd name huh?). After the meeting we asked Joe to come and join us – then we told him straight – he took too many risks with those wolves. And what was the point of having deputies if you did that?

We expected an argument but Joe agreed. I wish he hadn't – I like a good row, but that's the way it is. When you're ready for one you don't get it. But anyway Joe and us deputies agreed that in future all of us would be part of the plan. And we would not allow Joe to be left on his own without protection. We didn't want to lose our sheriff.

It was a good job we agreed that, because that bunch of wolves may have left but there were plenty others around. Maybe not quite as bad but they didn't stop coming just because one lot had been warned off. But Joe made us change our ways of doing things. He said that wild animal had a right to live too – you can't just go around killing everything. So he would go off and talk to the bears and the wolves that came prowling around. This time we weren't so far away and Joe never got quite so close. The warning mostly worked and where it didn't a few shots in the air gave 'em the message.

All that was nearly ten years ago. I was just a kid then; the youngest deputy the County had ever had. Mind you I had to fit it in around school and running errands. Since then the Mayor has stood down and there has been an election. And Joe Wolf was persuaded to stand. Well he won, and he's been Mayor for four years now. He lives in the Mayor's house in the smart area of town, but he often comes over to see me at the sheriff's office and we talk over old times.

You see I'm the sheriff now. I got the badge and the waistcoat, the cowboy hat and the belt with the fake guns But I do wish we hadn't knocked the bottom out of them high boots. I had to buy a new pair and they're nowhere near as good.

Sometimes I have to call in the Mayor to help me out, especially when it comes to bears and wolves. He's much better at dealing with them than I am. Other times he comes over and stays the night, sleeps out on the mat in the office. I don't sleep in the cell anymore but in the bedroom out back.

Since he's been Mayor – Joe has been encouraging everyone to plant more fruit and vegetables, and he's made sure there's always an alternative to meat on the school lunch menu. He's also done something about guns. Well there were an awful lot around. Everyone said they needed a gun in the house for protection. But Joe said the reason we needed protection was because everyone had guns. So he got a law passed cutting down the numbers.

Last year some people wanted to change the name of the town. They said what about Wolverton but we found there was already a town of that name. So someone suggested Wolverhamton but the same applied. There was a big list in the end including Wolfcote, Wolferlee, Wolfsburg. But Joe said I'm only one wolf – why do you want to change the name?

People said because we respect you.

Joe said, 'Well change it when you stop killing things if you respect me that much.'

Well they didn't respect him that much. Cus they still kill pigs and sheep and such like, and no one's talked much about changing the town name since. But they had another idea – and I liked that one better. Some people collected money for a statue. It was to be of a wolf standing on its hind legs wearing a cowboy hat and all the gear, and its front paws about to draw on its six-guns.

They wanted to put it right in the middle of the town. Except some of them wanted to do it when Joe was dead. I thought that was crazy. Why shouldn't he enjoy a statue of himself too? And I made a big fuss about it and got other people to complain as well.

In the end we wore them down and they got it made by this sculptor. He worked on it for months. Then there was all the palaver about what to write underneath it. Some said 'Joe', some said 'Joe Wolf'.

In the end I persuaded 'em what it should be. Well I knew him better than most.

And so come the unveiling the whole town was there, all dressed in their best. The band was playing, and along comes Joe in his Mayor's outfit, wearing his chain of office. Then he pulls the string. And away comes the curtain and shows everyone the statue of Joe as he was when was sheriff. And underneath, engraved in big letters it says:

The (almost) Good Wolf

Even Joe had a laugh at that.

The
(almost)
Good Wolf

ALSO BY DEREK SMITH

Frances Fairweather — Demon Striker!

Frances is an ace football player so obsessed with the game that her father and teacher ban her from playing with the girls' team. So Frances tries to join a local boys' team, the Tigers, but Stan, the Manager, doesn't believe in girls playing football and sends her packing. Then Frances has her great idea: by getting the right clothes and practising in her bedroom she becomes Frank, a tough macho boy, who the Tigers do take on. Within a few weeks she has become their top goal-scorer. But it isn't so easy pretending to be a boy. What started out as fun becomes a struggle, on and off the field, between the girl she is and the boy she plays.

Funny, clever and wonderfully credible, through football this book examines identity. It asks what is a boy?, what is a girl? — and the answers aren't as obvious as they at first seem.

For readers nine and upwards.

'A witty tale which deals with obsessions, ambitions and the problems of boy-girl identity as you are growing up'
LIVERPOOL ECHO

'A satisfying story, a story with considerable depths'
SCHOOL LIBRARIAN

'A very funny and almost believable book'
BOOKS FOR KEEPS

Published by Faber & Faber
ISBN 0-571-17451-5

ALSO BY DEREK SMITH

Hard Cash

What would you do if you found quarter of a million pounds?

When it happens to Shorty and Warby they give in to temptation and keep their find. Warby has dreams of owning a circus, while Shorty wants to leave their run-down estate and be someone. But holding on to their cash is easier said than done. Even spending it is a problem, with shopkeepers suspicious of thirteen-year-old boys brandishing twenty-pound notes. And it doesn't help having a nosy sister, who is too clever by half, either. Shorty is desperate: someone has to come up with a plan – and fast!

At once dramatic and wildly funny, this action-packed story suggests that money may cause more problems than it solves…

'High comedy but a classic morality none the less'
THE OBSERVER

'This is a tale red-hot with social realism'
THE GUARDIAN

*'Subtleties here to put alongside the brisk action,
the excitement and suspense'*
JUNIOR BOOKSHELF

Published by Faber & Faber
ISBN 0-571-17167-2